Solstice Burn

A Club Altura Romance Novella

Kym Grosso

Copyright © 2015 by Kym Grosso
All rights reserved. No part of this publication may be reproduced, distributed, or transmitted in any form or by any means, including photocopying, recording, or other electronic or mechanical methods, without the prior written permission of the publisher, except in the case of brief quotations embodied in critical reviews and certain other noncommercial uses permitted by copyright law.

MT Carvin Publishing, LLC
West Chester, Pennsylvania

Editor: Julie Roberts
Formatting: Polgarus Studio
Cover Design: LM Creations
Cover Model: Stuart Reardon
Photographer: Rick Day

DISCLAIMER
This book is a work of fiction. The names, characters, locations and events portrayed in this book are a work of fiction or are used fictitiously. Any similarity to actual events, locales, or real persons, living or dead, is coincidental and not intended by the author.

NOTICE
This is an adult erotic paranormal romance book with love scenes and mature situations. It is only intended for adult readers over the age of 18.

ACKNOWLEDGMENTS

~My husband, Keith, for encouraging me to write and supporting me in everything I do, and for our many fun vacations and adventures in the Caribbean that gave me inspiration for this story.

~Julie Roberts, editor, who spent hours reading, editing and proofreading Solstice Burn. You've done so much to help and encourage me over the past two years. As with every book, I could not have done this without you!

~My Alpha readers, Rochelle and Maria, who help give me such important feedback and insight during the editing process. You both are awesome!

~My dedicated beta readers, Elena, Gayle, Denise, Janet, Jessica, Jerri, Kelly, Leah, Laurie, Stephanie, and Rose for beta reading. I really appreciate all the valuable feedback you provide.

~LM Creations, cover artist, for designing Solstice Burn's sexy cover.

~Stuart Reardon, cover model, for another amazing image.

~Love N. Books, for image acquisition.

~ Rick Day, for image photography.

~Nicole, Indie Sage PR, for helping me with promotion and supporting my books.

~Gayle, my admin, who is one of my biggest supporters and helps to run my street team. I'm so thankful for all of your help!

~My awesome street team, for helping spread the word about the Immortals of New Orleans series and my new erotic contemporary romance Altura series. I appreciate your support more than you could know! You guys are the best. You rock!

Chapter One

Chase checked his oxygen and gave a thumbs up to his scuba partner, Evan. He knew he could have pushed deeper, but without his team, he erred on the side of safety. Chase Abbott, a wealthy executive at Emerson Industries, always brought his love of adventure to the forefront of his business; enhancing extreme sporting technologies, products and services to be utilized for both private enjoyment and government contracts. A trained biologist, his specialty focused on deep sea diving. Exploring uncharted locations always brought the possibility he'd discover unique materials that could be used for further research and development.

Deep in the abyss of the hole, he scraped at the wall, collecting a rock sample. While it was illegal for tourists to touch or otherwise harm the ecosystem, as a scientist he'd been granted permission to remove the tiny fragments. He glanced to Evan, who pointed to a bull shark that had come around to check out the invaders in his environment. Chase calmly bagged his specimen, and held his knife firmly. While shark attacks were rare, caution was his friend. Chase knew that this particular species could be aggressive. They both eyed the spectacular creature as it circled. He admired the massive beast, but was relieved when it swam away into the darkness, having satisfied its curiosity.

Chase signaled to Evan, letting him know they should begin their slow ascent. At a depth of a hundred and forty feet, they'd gone considerably further than most recreational divers. They'd taken the tour excursion from the resort, slipping the captain a few hundred extra to tag along and conduct their dive alone.

After a slow ascension, taking time for decompression stops, Chase surfaced and peeled his mask away. He bobbed in the water and waited on Evan who followed. He checked his surroundings, noting the boat to his right and the group of snorkelers swimming toward it. An unusual splash caught his attention, and he scanned the open sea behind him, expecting to see a breaching fish. Instead, he spied flailing arms bursting through the waves, then disappearing back into the ocean.

Chase flipped on his mask, quickly locating the victim. Her long brunette braid swished like a stalk of kelp and he reached around her torso, bringing her upward. She gasped for air as they broke through the water.

"You okay?" he asked, thanking God she hadn't managed to drown herself. She nodded her head yes but didn't speak.

It always amazed him how many tourists would go

snorkeling, expecting it to be easy. Instead of practicing in a pool, they'd impulsively choose the resort tour, experiencing it for the first time out in open water. Neophytes often found breathing through the snorkel challenging. Inexperience with strong currents and adverse interactions with wildlife were common causes of death.

As he reached the boat, he carefully lifted the woman to the waiting crew. While it hadn't been his first time saving a fledgling swimmer, he had to admit he'd never rescued someone so beautiful. As she assured the captain she was okay, she glanced over to him, and their eyes locked. Mouthing the words, 'thank you,' she tightened her grip on the towel she'd been given. He gave her a small smile and she returned it but quickly averted her gaze. *She's shy*, he thought. Chase considered that with his many planned dives, he hadn't intended to socialize on his vacation, but the flicker in her eyes gave him reason to believe things had just gotten a whole lot more interesting than the rock sample he'd collected.

Chapter Two

First day at the resort and Penny had almost died. *Go snorkeling. It'll be fun*, the concierge had said. She should have known better than to think she should try something even remotely adventurous. She'd wanted to talk to the sexy stranger who'd rescued her, but was stopped short as they'd brought another victim onto the boat. Apparently, the newlyweds had decided skinny snorkeling was in order and the husband had scraped his bits on fire coral. He'd been laid out like a filleted fish, his testicles looking like bright red oranges. Penny had rushed to help his wife, by bagging ice and gathering their belongings. When they'd returned to shore, she'd helped them get back to the room, staying with them until the hotel nurse had arrived. Unfortunately, by the time she'd returned to the dock, her handsome scuba diver had vanished.

She recalled the long boat ride back to the resort, and how she'd stolen glances at his broad muscular chest. As he peeled his tanned, hardened body out of his wetsuit, nearly every woman on board took notice. She'd inwardly laughed, amused that her near death experience had been coupled with lust. After everything she'd been through with relationships, she knew damn well that she shouldn't be giving a second thought to a man. But when he'd smiled at her and pushed on his sunglasses, she found the sight of him impossible to resist. The temptation of a vacation fling seemed more and more appealing.

Returning to her room, Penny lounged on her balcony, contemplating her next big undertaking, nude sunbathing. She took a sip of her punch and thanked the rum gods. For the first time in over six months, she was beginning to relax, stress fading fast with each breath of sea air. She was thankful that her best friend, Tori, had talked her into taking a vacation. Six months ago, when she'd found her ex in bed with their local barista, he'd blamed her for his indiscretion, insisting she worked too much and his needs weren't met. It wasn't as if she could argue. His comments hadn't been far from the truth, but it wasn't as if rent in Manhattan was going to pay itself. After two years of seventy-hour work weeks, she'd finally earned the attention of the partners.

In the wake of her breakup, Tori had declared an intervention was in order. "All work and no play makes Penny a dull girl," she had teased in the most tactful way possible, insisting they take an all-girl holiday to Precioso Beach. Penny resisted the idea at first. While she'd never been conservative per se, she'd also never been to an au natural beach before and was nervous at the prospect. During the third blizzard of their harsh New York winter and several glasses of wine later, Penny had relented and agreed to a holiday at the hedonistic resort.

Five days of paradise. One day of almost dying and four more to go. She hoped she'd run into her tanned savior once again and manage not to do anything stupid.

"Great dive today, huh? The wall was killer," Chase commented, referring to the vertical face they'd descended.

"Hey, I'm just along for the ride, Dr. Abbott. You know…enjoying the flora and fauna," Evan joked.

"You mean the bull that was giving us the big eye?"

"I was thinking more about the mermaid you reeled in when you got to the surface," he joked.

"Yeah, she was something, huh? They should have them practice in the pool before going out. Everyone thinks it's easy until they're sucking water."

"I hear ya. She seemed to rebound quickly, though."

"Sure did." Chase adjusted his sunglasses, pecked away at his iPad, and attempted to appear nonchalant.

"Everything okay back at home?" Evan asked, shaking the sand out of his towel.

"Yeah, just sending Garrett an update and checking email. I'd like to go back to the hole again before we leave. Let's charter a boat next time."

"Sounds good. Listen, I'm going to the pool. You want

me to wait for you?"

"No, you go ahead without me. I'm going to pack these samples and overnight them. They can get started on the analysis before we get back. I'll catch up with you later."

"So you're not going to say anything about mermaid girl? No comments, like, 'hey, she's pretty hot?'" Evan laughed.

Chase glanced at Evan, considering his answer. His friend knew him well enough to know when he was interested in a woman, but he wasn't ready to show his cards. He hadn't stopped thinking of the beautiful woman he'd rescued. If it were not for the guy with the flaming nuts, he'd have used the opportunity to ask her to dinner. Cockblocked by a honeymooner, he'd been forced to observe her from across the deck. After they'd docked, his lovely little snorkeler had gone off with the wife, helping them get back to their room.

Chase knew he shouldn't let himself become distracted by a woman. It wasn't as if he'd come to Precioso to play. But in the course of a few hours, it had become difficult to think about coral and shells. The only specimen he was interested in studying was the brunette he'd met out at sea.

"Depends," Chase replied, his eyes on the screen, concealing his feelings.

"On what?"

"First of all, most people just come to places like this as a one-fer. Some big excitement in their boring lives." He closed his tablet cover and set it on the stand next to the lounge.

"And your point is?"

"My point is that I don't even know her. Let's say I pursue her. It's not going to turn into anything."

"And? What's wrong with a little one night stand action? You think too much."

"Don't pull your playboy shit with me. Did it ever occur to you that maybe I get tired of that?" Chase sighed, reached for a tube of suntan lotion and flipped the cap open. "Besides, just because she's pretty to look at, that doesn't mean we're going to hit it off."

It had become a challenge for him to find someone who shared his adventurous interests. Within the confines of their exclusive club, Altura, Chase and Evan explored their drive to push harder and further into the world of extreme sports. Money was never a consideration as they tested each other's limits, flirting with death regularly. One person's threshold for risk could far exceed or far disappoint the expectations of another. Within Altura, however, they understood and played hard, with little regard to societal expectations. Considering the mermaid had almost killed herself attempting to snorkel, he suspected they'd have little in common.

"Maybe you just need to relax, Chase. It's not like you have to fuck her, for Christ's sake. Have a few cocktails. Some dinner. Dance a little. It's not like we've got a hard deadline. This is an exploration trip. We already bagged some good stuff today. You need to lighten up."

"Maybe," Chase conceded.

"If you're not interested, maybe I should go looking for her…"

"Fuck off." Chase glared at him.

"See? Someone is interested. All it took was a little competition to wake that limp dick of yours." Evan grabbed his gear and slung it over his shoulder. "I always loved brunettes."

"Stay away from the mermaid," Chase ordered, hurling the sunscreen at his friend.

The suite door slammed shut, and Chase considered his next move. As long as his lovely little fish was still on the island, he knew he'd have a hard time resisting. As he thought about her, he couldn't stop the picture that formed in his mind. With her braid wrapped tight around his fist, he slammed into her from behind. His dick jerked at the thought, and he knew right then he'd be fantasizing about an encounter for the rest of his days. Chase walked to the window and took a deep breath, trying to clear the image from his mind. But as he caught sight of the distinctive silhouette of his mystery woman on the beach, he realized his decision had already been made.

Chapter Three

Penny sighed and studied her face in the mirror. After the morning incident, she wasn't sure she had it in her to go naked on a beach. But after dosing herself with a few glasses of liquid courage, she'd bravely stripped and wrapped the sarong around her breasts. She wished she could be more like Tori, who'd simply gone off wearing nothing but a smile. But she reasoned that she wasn't going to waste her vacation sitting in the hotel room. It wasn't every day she got a day off, let alone five whole days on a tropical island.

By the time she got down to the beach, she noted that almost all the chairs had been taken. Spying a lounger near a palm tree, she waved to the towel attendant. Reggae music blared from the pool area, and Penny was certain that was where she'd find her friend. But unlike Tori, she preferred the solitude of the sand and planned on reading.

As beach staff covered her seat, she fiddled with the top of her wrap. She gave him a small smile when he finished, thanking him for his quick work. Deciding there was no time like the present, she quickly disrobed, her breasts bared. Penny wasn't sure what she thought would happen next but was relieved that not one person gave her a second glance as she settled onto the chaise face down. Bravely she lifted her gaze, pleased that nothing but a bird flying by stopped to stare at her.

Losing herself in her book, Penny read for over an hour until she was too hot to continue. She gingerly pushed upward, and spied an available raft at the edge of the surf. Dragging it into the ocean, her toes sank into the soft sand and she began to forget that she wasn't wearing a suit. All at once, she submerged herself into the cool water, a welcome relief from the scorching sun.

Hoisting herself onto the raft, she lay flat, relaxing as the gentle waves rocked her like a baby. Penny inhaled the calming scent of seawater, and her thoughts wandered to the handsome scuba diver, with the hopes she'd run into him on the island. Drifting in and out of sleep, she indulged in the fantasies she only had the courage to fulfill in her dreams.

A soft bump alerted her that she'd gone to the edge of the roped-in swimming area. Her eyes blinked open and her heart stopped as she caught sight of her rescuer floating on the raft next to her. Bare save for her hat, she stared into his gorgeous ice-blue eyes.

"Um…sorry," she stammered. Reaching her hands into the water, she paddled, in an attempt to get away. She glanced down and noticed her traitorous nipples were peaked at attention for the attractive stranger. Her already sun-kissed cheeks turned a deeper shade of red. "I fell asleep."

"It's okay; these things always seem to drift together eventually," he drawled.

"This is my first time," she explained.

"Hmm…so you're a virgin?" He laughed.

"A virgin? Not exactly, but this is my first time visiting here…to a place like this, anyway."

"How're you feeling? You had a bit of a scare today."

"I'm good. Thanks again for saving me." She gave him a small smile, recalling how she'd flailed about in the water. "The water got a bit rough and then I swallowed it. The next thing you know, I was going under. Thank God you were there."

"Snorkeling can be dangerous," he noted. "The guides should have kept a better eye on you."

"It was my fault. I can't believe I did that," she sighed. "Even a child can snorkel."

"You'd think it would be easy, but let's just say you aren't the first person I've seen have an accident."

"Sorry I didn't get a chance to thank you. I went back to look for you," she confessed. *Stop talking, Penny. He just said you're not the first fool he's rescued. Just because he's hotter than hell. Act casual.* "I, um, was helping. That guy on the boat. Did you see that?"

"Yeah I did. Can't imagine the rest of his honeymoon's going so well."

"I never knew that could happen." Penny attempted to keep her eyes trained on his, trying desperately not to stare at his muscular body. Well hidden behind her tinted glasses, she doubted he'd be able to see where her line of vision traveled. Still, she wasn't taking any chances, and concentrated on his face.

"Fire coral's painful. It's not so much of a coral, really. It's actually an animal."

"I'm sorry, what?"

"The guy on the boat. He must have snared himself on the stuff. It's more of a jellyfish, really. Stings really bad. Can last for a few weeks, even. Nasty."

"You seem to know a lot about..."

He reached for her raft, and she startled. "You don't mind, do you? Just didn't want you to drift away before we got a chance to introduce ourselves."

"Um, no, I guess not. I'm Penelope Travis. But my friends call me Penny." She lost control, her eyes traveling over his shoulders. The tanned corded muscles of his back streamed down into perfectly carved glutes. He rested his chin on his crossed arms, his pecs bulging as he flexed to adjust his body.

"Chase. Chase Abbott." He gave her a broad smile. "So, this is your first time at Precioso, huh?"

"Yeah, my friend, Tori...she's here with me. She talked me into coming."

"This is my first time here, too, although I have been to beaches like this one before."

"You have?"

"Don't sound so surprised. It's fairly common in other parts of the world. Even in California we've got a few." He winked.

"I think there might be one in New Jersey," she offered, having heard a rumor from a friend. She'd been too chicken to even consider going.

"You east coast?"

"New York City. You?"

"San Diego."

"You sound like you're from the south."

"Grew up in North Carolina but I've lived in California for years now." Chase tugged on her drifting raft, bringing her closer. He adjusted it so that he faced her perpendicularly.

"I, um, I was raised in New Jersey but I've lived in New York...ever since grad school." Penny stumbled over her words as his face came within a few inches of her breasts. She cursed as her beaded tips swelled in response. Hoping to squelch her arousal, she reached into the water and dribbled it onto her body.

"So tell me, Penny, what do you do in New York City?" A broad smile crossed his face, and he brought his sunglasses down over his eyes, obscuring his gaze.

"I'm a lawyer."

"I see. Large firm?"

"It's good-sized. McNally, Reeves and Sullivan."

"Corporate law?"

"Yeah, how'd you know? Have you heard of them?" Penny prayed like hell he hadn't. Her boss would have a conniption if he found out she'd gone to this kind of resort. He was a born and bred, old money conservative, and there was no room for mistakes. Until now, she'd been the epitome of the perfect employee as he groomed her for junior partner. Her career would be over faster than she could say piña colada if he ever found out where she went on vacation.

"I know of them," he said, not offering any information.

"So what do you do when you're not rescuing people in the ocean?" Penny paused and took a deep breath. "I noticed you weren't snorkeling with the rest of us."

"Many things, but for the purposes of this trip, I'm here doing some research. Where we dove today, there's a hole."

"A hole?"

"Yeah, it's like a cliff."

"That sounds scary."

"All part of the fun, darlin'."

"I'm not sure I could ever be that adventurous," she stated. *Scuba diving?* No way that was ever happening, considering she'd almost killed herself by attempting to snorkel.

"You never know. Sometimes we don't know our limits until we push them."

"I'm not sure that's true," she countered.

"Today, for example. Have you ever snorkeled?" he asked.

"Well, no. But look how that turned out." Penny reached for his raft and he smiled in response.

"Fair enough. But you came here. To an adult resort…one with a nude beach."

"Yes, but..."

"Have you ever been completely naked in front of a total stranger?"

"No," she whispered.

"But you are now, aren't you? And you're talking to me. We just established a connection, discussed where we live, what we do for a living."

"Touché."

"So you did push a limit...one you thought you had. It's how we learn, grow. Hopefully, we don't get hurt...have fun doing it. Tell me, Penny, do you have fun?"

"I don't know. Maybe not as much as I'd like to. I want to have fun, but it's not like I..." Penny hesitated. She was reluctant to admit the truth. "I don't know. I guess I don't usually have fun. I mean, there's just not time."

"How about now?"

"What do you mean?"

"Are you having fun?"

"Yes." Penny laughed. As she shifted on her raft, it pitched, and she fell toward him. His hand reached for her belly, steadying her.

"You okay?" he asked.

"Yes, sorry. I'm such a klutz today. Geez." The heat of his palm sizzled on her stomach and an ache grew between her legs. Her hand moved to his but he slid it away. In that moment, she wanted him. He was a total stranger, she knew, but it didn't matter.

"Have dinner with me tonight."

"I...I have to check with Tori."

"Bring her, then. I'll invite Evan."

"Well, I don't know if I can answer for Tori. I mean, no...yes..." Penny inwardly cringed at how inarticulate she sounded. *Sweet baby Jesus, Penny, get your shit together.* She took a deep breath and smiled. "I'd love to have dinner with you."

"Pick you up at eight? What's your room number?" he asked, like a wolf who was about to eat his prey.

"I'll meet you there," she countered. The tropical paradise might have stolen most of her brain cells, but her New York roots reminded her to be cautious. No matter how much her body told her 'hell yes,' she wanted to get to know him *with* her clothes on.

"The Bistro, eight o'clock. I'll meet you at the front entrance."

"Sounds good," Penny agreed.

As he slid off his raft, he shot her a sexy smile that sent quivers straight through to her pussy. Penny sighed, watching him exit the ocean. Like a rippling Greek god, he emerged from the surf, water droplets rolling off his bronze torso. Unconsciously, her hands moved to her breast as she recalled his palm on her skin. A crashing wave jarred her thoughts, and she cursed under her breath. She toppled off her float into the sea, washing away his touch. The cool water should have put a damper on the erotic fantasies that had formed in her mind. But as she dove under, it was of little consequence. It was far too late to stifle the delicious image of his head between her legs.

Chapter Four

Chase took a draw of his beer and recalled the brief interlude with Penny. A natural beauty, her long dark brown hair trailed over her tanned shoulders. She'd blushed as soon as they'd started speaking. While she was a novice to the au natural beach experience, he detected a streak of adventure just waiting to be discovered. When she'd drizzled sea water over her full breasts, he'd found it difficult to concentrate.

He'd laughed, thinking it had been a good thing he'd been lying on his stomach when he'd found her floating. Never in his life had he let himself get aroused on a nude beach, but the more he'd talked with her, the harder he became. He'd deliberately taken his time leaving the ocean, careful not to turn around. Grabbing his nearby towel off the chaise, he concealed his erection and cursed his amateurish behavior.

When she'd nearly fallen off her raft, he hadn't meant to put his hand on her without permission. As if he'd touched fire, he'd quickly removed it. Sitting at the bar, he glanced at his palm. Her silky skin fresh in his mind, his cock jerked in response. He blamed it on his lack of sex, aware that he'd been preoccupied for months with his research. But after talking to Penny at the beach, he was certain the only solution to quelling his arousal was to be inside the lovely counselor.

Chase's attention was drawn to laughter outside the restaurant. He glanced to the veranda where he caught a glimpse of Penny talking with a woman. He smiled as his eyes drank in the sight of her. Even more gorgeous than he'd remembered, she wore a blue print sundress, its plunging neckline exposing a hint of her cleavage. She noticed him, giving a wide smile and a shy wave.

"Penny," he greeted her as she approached, noting her friend had disappeared.

"Hey there." She nervously pushed a stray lock behind her ear and scanned the open air café.

"Are we dining alone?" He hadn't meant to say it so enthusiastically but he failed to conceal his excitement.

"Yep. Seems Tori's hooked up with a group that's going off resort. What about your friend?"

"Evan? Seems he had a tad too much rum at the pool. He's sleeping it off." He offered his hand, pleased when she placed her palm in his. "Shall we? I have a table."

In a romantic location overlooking lush gardens, Chase

and Penny laughed throughout their meal, keeping their conversation light and enjoyable. She told him about her life in New York City, speaking in a self-deprecating manner about her position within the law firm. And while he was unable to tell her the details of his own projects or company, she appeared interested in his diving experiences and knowledge of the ocean.

By the end of dinner, he'd grown even more attracted to Penny Travis, and it caused him concern, given they had no future. After meeting her, however, he suspected things might never be the same.

They toasted, and Chase nodded to the band who'd begun to play. Without answering, she smiled and took his hand. They made their way to the dance floor and he laughed in satisfaction as she fell into his arms. He'd never been a dancer but with Penny, the only thing he could think of was the rush of excitement he felt every time their bodies came together. As the song slowed, she laid her head upon his shoulder, her coconut-scented hair teasing his senses. They swayed as one to the sultry rhythm, his erection brushing against her belly.

She smiled up at him, and he shoved away a pang of guilt, knowing it could only be a fling. He swore to himself that he'd talk to her before they made love. If there was one thing Chase believed in, it was honesty. He didn't play games with others, not even when it would clearly benefit him or his own goals. As she brought their clasped hands to her side, and his thumb grazed her breast, he knew they'd better talk soon.

Chapter Five

Penny's heart caught as she danced with Chase and she realized how much she enjoyed spending the evening with him. They'd spent several hours talking, and she couldn't recall ever having such an intense connection with someone she'd only just met. Captivated by his charismatic personality, she'd fallen under his spell. Like old lovers, they engaged in an easy banter, but their attraction sizzled hotter than the sun itself. Earlier in the day, she'd expected the sexual tension she'd experienced in the ocean would wane, proving her libido wrong. But as the night proceeded, she'd fantasized about making love to him.

In his arms, Penny breathed in his masculine scent, and deliberately ground her body against his erection. Within Chase's safe embrace, she reveled in her sexuality, knowing he was every bit as turned on as she was. As his lips pressed to her collarbone, she moaned, yearning for him to touch her. The desire to be consumed by her handsome savior far outweighed her need for logical explanations of why she shouldn't be with him. No longer did she wish to dance, she wanted him…now…on her, inside her.

"Chase," she breathed. Penny lifted her head from his chest, and her eyes locked on his. As his palm cupped her cheek, her world stalled on its axis.

"I like you, Penny." Chase glanced to her lips, leaning toward her, but stopped within inches of kissing her. He gave a small smile, his eyes darting to the ocean and back to her. "How do you feel about moonlit walks on the beach?"

"I don't think I've ever done that," she admitted.

"You don't know what you're missing." Chase took her hand in his, leading her off the dance floor.

Penny wondered why he hadn't kissed her and she grew concerned that what she thought was growing between them had all been in her own head. When they reached the beach, she watched as he kicked off his shoes and rolled up his white linen pants. She began to walk toward him, her sandals filling with sand.

"Hold on," Chase said.

When he knelt in front of her, she smiled as he gently removed her shoes and set them aside. He locked his eyes on hers and ran his hands up the back of her calves. She shivered as he grazed them upward, his strong fingers pressing against her thighs.

"You have beautiful legs," he began.

"Thank you." Penny laughed, embarrassed. She swiveled her head to see if anyone was looking.

"Does this make you uncomfortable?" He smiled.

She went still as his hands moved to her hips, his fingers slipping underneath the strings of her panties.

"Chase…"

"Or are you aroused?"

"I…there could be people watching." As he tugged her panties down her legs, she reached to steady herself on his shoulders.

"There are things you don't know about me. The things I like. Risk…taking chances."

"I can see that," she giggled as he lifted each of her feet to remove her underwear.

"Is that something you might be interested in exploring with me?" he asked, stuffing them into his pocket.

"Maybe. That sounds like a commitment and we don't have much time," she hedged.

He stood, brushing his hands up the sides of her legs, pulling the fabric up to her hips. Her heart raced as he exposed her skin.

"Penny." His tone grew serious. "I can't promise you more than the time we have here together. If we lived closer…"

"Fair enough. But we just met, so who knows what the week will bring?" She placed her hands over his, and brushed them away. Reaching for her shoes, she picked them up and walked toward the surf. Penny gave him a flirty smile, going slowly enough that he'd easily catch up to her.

"True. But you've given me the most wonderful souvenir."

"Listen, Chase, you need to know…I didn't come on vacation thinking I'd meet someone." When he reached for her hand, she laced her fingers with his. "I work a lot. I know the office stories I told you over dinner make it seem enjoyable, but I can assure you that most of the time what I do is not fun. I want to make partner someday."

"That's a good goal."

"So I guess what I'm saying is that it's not like I have any big expectations about what's happening here. I mean, I like you…a lot. But you and I…"

"We lead different lives."

"It seems like you travel a lot."

"Yeah, I do."

"It would never work, I get that." As she said the words that defined the situation, her heart squeezed. It was true she hadn't expected anything, but every second she spent with him, she was becoming addicted. If they made love, she guessed it would be even harder to say goodbye forever.

"Wait here," he told her.

"Um, okay." Penny dipped her toes in the surf as he ran up toward the path. When he returned, she grinned, watching him lay several towels onto the sand.

"Come sit." It was an order that sent tingles down her body. She obeyed and relaxed as he put an arm around her. "I know we just have a few days, but I want to get to know you better. At the same time, I don't want to hurt you."

"You won't hurt me," she protested, aware she was

lying to herself. "But it does seem like you enjoy risky behavior."

"Diving to the depths I do is dangerous, but is it worth the risk? Hell yeah, because it's exciting. This is who I am. It's my life. I know you're not really like that, but I can teach you."

Penny considered his words. His fingers guided her chin to meet his gaze.

"How far do you want to go with me, darlin'?"

"In a week, I'll go back to working fourteen-hour days." She sighed, her lips tense as she expressed the reality of the situation. "How far will I go? With you?" She adjusted her body so she faced him. As she answered, she didn't hesitate. Even if she could only taste happiness for a few days, she'd take it. "All the way. I want it all."

"This place is special….you're special." Chase reached for the spaghetti straps that held her dress up and slid them over her shoulders.

"What are you…?" Despite her concern that they'd be watched, she sat still as he gently pulled down the fabric, her nipples hardening as the air rushed over them.

"You're beautiful." He grazed the back of his fingers over her firm tips and she exhaled.

"I…I've never done anything like this."

"I want to make love to you, Miss Travis," he said, never taking his eyes off her.

"Here?"

"Yes, here." He smiled.

"But…are you serious? Here on the beach?" The

prospect of being watched should have disgusted her, she knew. But the rush of knowing it could happen only served to make it all the more exciting. Penny jumped slightly as his hands cupped her breasts.

"Yes. Here," he repeated, his lips mere inches from hers.

"Yes." Penny shifted in an attempt to assuage the painful ache between her legs. She'd never wanted a man so badly in her life.

As he captured her lips, she opened to him. His tongue swept into hers and she returned his soft kiss. Gently, he made love to her mouth, and the startling realization hit her that this person she'd met, the man who'd saved her, soothed her vulnerable heart. Closed and cautious, she'd long dismissed the idea that she'd develop an attraction for someone. Chase had taken her off guard, her body and mind welcomed him into her life.

She supposed she'd expected a quickie, being that they were on the beach, but this man was in no hurry. Just as his words had drawn her into his web, his slow sensual kiss drove her mad with desire. She reached for his chest, grazing her palm down the hard expanse of his pecs. Her hand slid under his loose shirt, and she thumbed over his raised tip. He groaned in response, and as she moved down toward his pants, he clamped his hand over her wrists. Laying her back onto the towel, he placed soft kisses along her collarbone. Breathless, she panted as he held her arms over her head, his soft lips tasting her skin.

"Darlin', you sure you want to do this? Because I don't

think I can resist you."

"Yes," she whispered.

Chase pulled down the fabric of her dress, and Penny gasped, the warmth of his mouth teasing her nipple. As he took it between his teeth and flicked it with his tongue, her pussy throbbed in arousal. She writhed underneath him, attempting to get him to relieve her need. But his attention lingered at her breast, painfully escalating her anticipation.

"Beautiful," she heard him say right before he released her wrists, and shoved her dress up over her head. She reached for his shirt, which she deftly unbuttoned and removed.

"Let me see you." With his pants still on, he gazed upon her.

Aware that she was fully nude out on the darkened beach, Penny's breath quickened. Lights flickered in the distance, the soft notes of the steel band beating into the night. Her focus was brought back to Chase as he spread her thighs wide open. The ocean breeze did little to cool the heat between her legs.

"Chase." She feigned protest. *Good girls don't do these things*, she thought to herself.

"Darlin'." He paused. Dragging his thumbs into her folds, he pulled them apart so he could view his prize. "I've been waiting for this all night."

"Ahh," she cried.

Any remaining doubts disappeared as the first lash of his tongue grazed over her clit. Her hips tilted up to meet his delightful assault. She reached between her legs and dug her fingers into his hair, guiding him to her. Quivering, she pumped her hips upward. Her eyes closed, every cell in her body awakened.

"Holy shit, Chase," Penny said as he plunged two thick digits into her channel. He curled the pads of his fingers along her ridged band of nerves, driving her orgasm to the surface.

"That's it. I can feel you," he spoke into her lips. He took her hooded nub between his lips and sucked, flicking his tongue over it.

Penny's eyes flew open, her climax slamming into her. She came hard, his lips unrelenting on her pussy. Panting, she thrashed her head, shocked at the ecstasy he'd brought.

He rose, pressing his lips to hers, sweeping his tongue into her mouth. Tasting herself, she sucked his lips and reached to free his cock. Taking it into her hands, she stroked it hard, sliding her thumb over its weeping slit. She went to brush him over her clit but he stopped her.

"Condom," he breathed.

"Yes, of course," she agreed, panting. Penny couldn't believe she'd almost had unprotected sex. *Shit. What the hell am I thinking?* While she was on the pill, she cursed her stupidity, aware of the possible consequences.

She heard the sound of the foil tearing and within seconds his hard tip pressed at her entrance, focusing her attention. Penny gasped, his cock spearing into her, stretching her wide. She breathed through the twinge of pain, her channel opening to accept him. As she lifted her lids, she caught him watching her.

"You're stunning tonight. Did I tell you that? The moonlight on your face…"

Penny smiled and held his gaze, aware that whatever was happening between them felt like they'd known each other forever. Lost in the moment, she'd forgotten about everything in her life, her ex, her job; and for the first time in years, she felt alive.

"Jesus, you feel so good," he whispered, slowly retreating and pumping into her.

"Oh my God…" Penny wrapped her legs around him as he filled her, meeting his slow thrusts. Her head tilted off the towel into the sand as his lips brushed behind her ear, causing gooseflesh to ripple down her arms. His tongue lingered at her collarbone, and she arched her back, her breasts crushing against his chest. "Chase."

"You like this?" He laughed, continuing to kiss and suck at her neck while he rocked into her.

"There…harder." Penny's breath quickened as he slowly tantalized her clit. Raising her hips, she sought more friction. He grazed his pelvis against hers, and she shuddered beneath him. Her pussy contracted, her legs clenching him tighter. "I'm going to come…Chase…please…"

"Hmm…not yet."

Penny squealed as he rolled over onto his back, and brought her with him. She hadn't thought he could be inside her any deeper, but she was wrong. Her swollen nub slid down against him, his shaft embedded to the hilt.

"Let me see you," he told her. Placing his palms on her shoulders, he guided her upward to ride him.

She moaned in protest as her lips left his chest, but complied. Her hair spilled forward, a satisfied grin on her face as she impaled herself on him.

"Ah, yeah...you feel so good," Chase groaned.

He reached for her breasts, and strummed his thumbs over her rigid nipples. Penny undulated her hips, her clitoris tingling in desire as it brushed over him. Rising above Chase, she slammed down onto him, his shaft plunging into her quivering channel.

"I've never seen a more beautiful creature," Chase cried out loud as she rode him hard.

"Ah...yes...fuck me," she demanded, as he pumped up into her. Reaching for his arms, she wrapped her hands around his wrists. "Touch me...please, Chase, please."

"Your wish is my command, princess...let me see that pussy of yours." His hand dropped from her breast to between her legs.

As he gave attention to her clit, circling it with the pad of his thumb, Penny fell forward, bracing her palm on the towel, her hair flowing onto his face. Her body lit on fire as his thick shaft pounded up into her. She mumbled his name over and over again, her climax claiming her. Shattering above him, she lost herself in the stranger who'd rescued her.

Chase gave her no quarter, plunging himself up into her core. He gripped her chin, guiding her mouth to his, nipping and sucking at her lips. With a loud grunt, he stiffened in release. Penny's lips brushed over his, as she heaved for breath. She pressed her body to his as he relented, removing his fingers from her wet cleft. The slight prick of his scruff-covered cheek wasn't nearly enough to remind her where she was. As if she'd died and gone to heaven, she lay atop him, purring as he caressed her back, his fingers trailing up into her mane.

"Penny…you're incredible."

"Chase…I've never…." Her words trailed off as she attempted to process the amazing experience she'd just shared with him.

Of all the things Penny had expected on vacation, she never thought she'd meet someone who could rock her world the way he'd done. As reality seeped into her mind, her heart constricted, aware she'd have to say goodbye in four days. Yearning to hold him a little closer, staving off the inevitable, she wrapped her hands around his neck and closed her eyes.

Wind chimes echoed in the distance, reminding her that they weren't alone. While reality beckoned, she gave in to her fantasy, content in his embrace, wishing she could stay there forever.

Chapter Six

Chase's heart pounded against his ribs as the last spasms tore through his body. Penny's warm breath teased his chest, and he held her tight, unwilling to release her. He relaxed, embracing her small form. Glancing up to the starry sky, he contemplated the disturbing emotion that churned in his chest. He knew he was in trouble. What was supposed to be a work vacation was turning into something much more complicated.

He was only going to be on the island a few more days, and when he left, whatever he and Penny had started would have to end. The fact that he'd started anything ate at him. Having come to an understanding before they'd had sex hadn't absolved him. Making love to her had been more of a spiritual experience, not just a one off like he'd planned. Although he'd pushed the envelope by making love to her on the beach, he wondered how well she'd understand the high risk activities in which he engaged.

She stirred in his arms, drifting in and out of sleep, and he pressed his lips to her forehead. Brushing a stray hair from her forehead, he studied the contours of her face. The moon shone bright, illuminating her swollen pink lips. The taste of them fresh in his mind, he started running through the scenarios.

He was a scientist at heart. Hard facts were impossible to ignore. She lived on the east coast, he lived on the west, two very different worlds. In the city that never sleeps, she led a fast-paced, high-pressure existence, whereas he reveled in his own laid back lifestyle. Far from the busy nine-to-five rut, he often relaxed on the beach in sunny California. Chase accomplished his research both in and out of the office, with the added perks of working from wherever he wanted whenever he wanted.

If he'd been working on any other project, he'd have followed the general guidelines of the scientific process, developing theories, experimenting, testing, until it either failed or he'd developed a viable technology that could be used and sold by Emerson Industries. Penny was a person, not a product, he knew. His nagging conscience told him it was wrong to continue seeing her, in the whimsical hope that he could find a solution to the issues he'd identified.

But as her soft hand reached for his face and she traced her forefinger over his bottom lip, what lay in his heart superseded any rational thoughts. Fascinated by the sensual woman in his arms, he couldn't let her go so easily. The drive to see where things would lead between them was overwhelming, despite his awareness of the obstacles that would keep them apart. With four days of vacation left, he needed more of Miss Travis.

"Chase," she whispered.

"Hmm…you okay?" He felt her shiver under his palm and realized it was becoming much too cool to stay on the beach. *Don't spend the night with her,* his mind warred with him. *Fuck it. I want her.* "Come back with me."

"What?" Penny pushed up onto his chest. She glanced to her exposed breasts and quickly covered them with her arm as if she'd forgotten where they were. Her eyes fell to their clothes, strewn on the sand. "I, um, should get dressed."

"Spend the night with me," he insisted. Chase knew he'd been given an out, but let it pass. He could have thanked her for the evening, taken her back to her room and been done with things.

"I don't know. Didn't you say you were here with someone?" Penny licked her lips and gave him a sheepish smile.

"Working, yeah. But we aren't staying in the same room. This isn't college," he joked. Chase brushed his knuckles gently over her cheek, his thumb gliding down her jaw. "Penny, I…I know we just met, but I'd like to spend time with you."

Sweet Jesus, I sound like a teenager. Chase inwardly cringed. He thought to correct his words, to tell her to forget it, but on the verge of becoming sorely inarticulate, he decided silence was the best policy.

"You sure you want me to come with you? You really don't have to ask me. I don't want this to be awkward. What I mean to say is that I don't expect anything. I know this is just kind of a vacation thing, but I won't be hurt if you aren't interested." Penny paused, glanced to his lips and back to his eyes.

"Did you have a good time tonight?"

"Of course. It was amazing. I don't think I've ever met anyone like you."

"Then it's settled. You're coming home with me." *Not home…your hotel room.*

"I don't want you to think I do this kind of thing all the time. I…I haven't dated in a long time. Not that this was a date," she said nervously.

"It was kind of a date…we talked, had dinner, danced. We also walked on the beach, kissed. I haven't dated in a long time either, but I think what we just did was a date." He laughed, and shifted, his softened cock slipping out of her.

"I guess." Penny broke contact with him.

"I'm out of practice, too, but I'm quite sure what we just had was a date." Chase studied her as she appeared to consider his argument. He stretched across the sand and handed her her dress. As she turned to pull it over her head, he observed that she once again retreated into modesty. She'd been wild and uninhibited earlier. With the heat of the moment passed, it was as if she struggled with letting go of her apprehensions. "Let's call this date number two."

"Okay, I accept your logic. It appears that we had a date. A very nice one." She giggled. "But going back to your room? How exactly is that a date?"

"It's a sleepover." Chase deftly removed his condom and disposed of it in a trash bin that rested against a palm tree.

"A sleepover, huh?"

"Yep. We'll have some food, something to drink." He slipped on his pants and snatched his shirt off the beach.

"Play games?"

"That's the spirit. I can think of a few I'd like to play with you." Chase closed the distance and took her hand in his. Helping her to her feet, he brought her palm to his cheek and kissed her wrist.

"Spin the bottle?"

"Too tame. I'm afraid I have much more wicked things in store for you, my lovely mermaid."

"Is that so?"

"Say yes."

"To your games?"

"To all of it." Chase pulled her into his embrace, wrapping his arm about her waist.

"Chase...I want to say yes." Penny smiled and her expression grew sultry, her lips nearing his.

"Say you'll come back with me."

"Yes," she whispered.

"Yes." Chase gave her a small smile as she acquiesced, and captured her lips with his.

Four days and he'd go home, he reminded himself. But as she moaned, relaxing into his arms and running her soft hands up his bare back, his possessive nature flared to life. He wanted her no matter the cost. Sweetly surrendering to his own instincts, he'd drown in the abyss of her warmth with no regrets.

Chapter Seven

Penny's thoughts swam with emotions she had never thought would surface on a vacation. It was crazy, she knew. As if she were sliding off a cliff, she'd lost her equilibrium, spinning toward the ground. But as Chase put his arm protectively around her shoulder, whispering sweet nothings, she'd stopped trying to regain control. Somewhere between making love to him and their walk back to his villa, she'd released her trepidation. For far too long she'd held on tight, wearing her professional mask for everyone around her. Here, in the hedonistic tropics, no one cared who she was or what she did. Chase encouraged her to be the free spirit that until now, she'd only dreamed of being.

She tried to work through in her mind how it could be possible to see him when the vacation ended. Penny knew she shouldn't go there, but when she'd lain quietly in his embrace, his skin on hers, she'd imagined dating Chase. The distance was a showstopper. Working long hours, she'd barely be able to see him, even if he actually lived in the city, let alone across the country.

When he'd asked her to go with him, she'd vacillated between hiding in her hotel room for the rest of the vacation or simply ignoring all reason, pretending that she'd discovered her next boyfriend. She'd love nothing more than to indulge, making love all night. But one brief encounter had already left her light headed, a tiny crack in her previously impenetrable heart cleaved open. His compelling argument had been difficult to resist, and within seconds she'd agreed to spend the night with him.

As he flicked on the lights in his villa, she took in her surroundings, realizing his accommodations were far more luxurious than anything she'd known existed at the resort. Like a condominium, the spacious foyer led to a living room and dining area. Through the open-aired, screened doors, the moonlight reflected off the waves.

"Come on in. Make yourself at home," he told her, picking up the phone. "I'm going to call room service and order some snacks."

"Thanks." Penny set her shoes down in the foyer and scanned the extravagant suite, white marble surfacing the floors. Its opulence caused her to wonder again about what Chase did and where he was employed.

Working in Manhattan, she was no stranger to the luxury her clients expected. Within the mahogany-paneled walls of her office, one could taste the power and affluence. But Penny, who'd just recently paid off her college loans, lived modestly but comfortably in her one bedroom apartment on the Upper East Side.

As Chase ordered their food, he gave her a smile, his gaze bringing warmth to her belly. The roar of the waves called to her and she walked out onto the lanai. She leaned her forearms onto the wooden railing and breathed in the sea air. Relaxation rippled through her despite the excitement, expecting they'd make love again.

"Cold?" she heard Chase ask.

Strong hands wrapped around her waist, the heat of his chest to her back. She weaved her fingers into Chase's hand, shivering as his soft lips brushed her temple.

"A little." As if they'd been lovers for years, she leaned back onto him, resting her arms over his.

"I've been neglecting my warming duties."

"I'm kind of sandy, too." She laughed.

"As am I."

Penny took a deep breath and exhaled.

"Regrets?"

"Oh no." She laughed. "I think sex on the beach is underrated."

"Definitely."

"People don't know what they're missing."

"Exactly. I like how you think, counselor."

"Hmm…don't call me that. Reminds me of work."

"Ah, I see. Shall I call you mermaid? I've been partial to thinking of you as one."

"Much better." She smiled. Penny didn't want anything to remind her of the real world that waited for her at home.

"Perhaps we should take a shower?"

"Are you trying to get me naked again?"

"Me? Nah? I'm just very interested in skin care."

"Skin care, huh?" She laughed.

"I'm very thorough, did I mention that? After all, I am responsible for your sandy state."

"I think it's only fair, then, that you take responsibility."

"I suppose I need to make sure to pay careful attention to all your delicate areas." He squeezed her tightly.

"I expect nothing less. I'm very dirty," she teased.

"Are you now?"

"Yes I am. I think you need to do something about it."

"You like to tease me, do you?" Chase spun her around in his arms, caging her against the rail.

"Maybe," she whispered with a coy smile. Her heart sped up as he leaned into her, his lips inches from hers.

"How about we get clean so we can start our sleepover?" He winked.

"What about room service?"

"They'll set it up for us."

"You sure?"

"You bet. Let's get going. I have a date with a mermaid and I can't wait a second longer."

As Chase led her by the hand into the villa, Penny felt breathless with anticipation. Larger than life and compelling, he was like a force of nature, pushing her to look within herself. Penny's stomach flipped as he glanced back to her and she knew in that moment that she'd have a hard time saying no to anything he proposed.

The hot spray pelted her face and she giggled as his slippery cock brushed against the small of her back. She turned her face to him and tilted her hair into the shower. Arching her back, she purposefully jutted her chest toward him.

"My little tease," he began. He twisted her back around, reaching to cup her breasts. Teasing her nipples into hard points, he gently bit her shoulder.

"Ah," she cried, the sweet pain spearing desire straight to her pussy.

"It's my job to clean you, remember?"

Penny exhaled sharply as he released her. Unsure of what he'd do next, she smiled as he worked shampoo into her hair.

"We're going to have a lot of fun playing tonight. I do enjoy water." His fingers scrubbed her scalp, and then worked to rinse out the bubbles. "You're spectacular when wet."

"I think you're the dirty boy, now." She laughed.

"The things you do to me."

"Have you always enjoyed the water?" she inquired.

"Seriously?"

"Seriously."

"Yeah, I've been around water ever since I was a kid."

"How'd you learn to scuba dive?" She squealed as his soapy hands glided down her shoulders to her fingertips.

"My parents used to take me to the Bahamas when I

was younger. My grandparents retired there. Pop taught me how to snorkel when I was ten."

"And the diving?"

"I didn't learn that until I was fifteen."

"And?"

"And what?"

"Ah…" Penny sighed as his fingers passed through her folds. "Hey now…I need to concentrate."

"Why would you ever want to do that?" He laughed.

"Because we're talking. Isn't that what happens at sleepovers?"

"I suppose."

"Why do you still dive?" Penny pressed. She slid around to face him. Her palms to his chest, she gently pushed him under the water. She pumped shampoo into her hands and reached up around his neck. Standing on her tiptoes, her fingers speared into his hair. While she worked the lather, she grazed her breasts against his chest.

"You're distracting," he breathed. "What?"

"Why do you still dive? What do you like about it?" she asked.

"It's like sex, darlin'. Until you do it, you don't know how good it can be and once you do it, you don't ever want to stop."

"Hmm…sounds pretty great." Penny laughed. "How about college? Where'd you go?"

"MIT."

"And?" Her voice sang as she soaped underneath his arms and down the flank of his sides.

"Short version. I got my doctorate. Filed a few scientific patents."

"Patents, huh?"

"Yeah, they're important for protecting intellectual property."

"I hear that's true," she joked. "You didn't tell me where you worked…"

"No I didn't, but I didn't think we were talking about work, remember?"

"Thank you for reminding me, sir. Duly noted." Penny's eyes met his and she smiled. Her fingers trailed down his body, tracing the v cut of his abs. Delving between his legs, her pinkies grazed the sides of his testicles. She gripped his erection, stroking it clean.

"Penny…"

"Hmm…something wrong, Dr. Abbott? Just returning the favor." Penny fisted him with one hand and cupped his balls with the other. She held his dick up into the spray, rinsing him clean. Her courage rose as she knelt before him and slowly licked its plump head.

"What are you doing, darlin'?" he asked.

She raised her gaze to his, the fire in his eyes burning hot. The quiet moment between them lingered as his crown passed through her lips, but as she took him all the way into her throat, his loud cry reverberated throughout the stone enclosure. His fingers plowed into her wet locks, and his head lolled back against the granite tiles. She dug her fingernails into his hardened glutes, allowing him to guide her as he fucked her mouth.

"Penny," he breathed, increasing his pace as he plunged into her.

"Hmm..."

"No, Penny...aw, shit. I'm gonna come...I don't want to..."

She heard his protest, aware that he'd grown concerned, but the urge to take him whole, to pleasure him the way he'd done to her, drove her. Sucking hard, Penny gripped his shaft, pumping him into her warmth. She dropped a hand between his legs, applying pressure to the soft stretch of nerves under his balls.

"I can't stop," she heard him cry as he spilled his seed into her mouth. He grunted, grasping her hair, heaving for breath. His briny essence rushed down over her tongue, and she suckled his cock, milking his spasms.

As she released him, he clasped her wrists, bringing her into his embrace. She smiled, satisfied with her task, elated to have given him the ecstasy he'd brought her.

"You're incredible," he whispered, still breathless from his orgasm.

"I love being with you." As she said the words, she thought perhaps she should restate her sentiment. But there was something refreshing about the brutal honesty of her statement that both cut and soothed her heart. It had been such a long time since she'd felt anything for any man, felt happy, and she meant what she'd said.

"Penny...I..."

"You don't need to say anything."

"I wasn't expecting..."

"Chase, it's okay. I'm not sure what it is…when I'm around you…" Her gaze fell to the floor, then returned to meet his. "I just feel like a different person."

"It's a good thing?" he asked with a small grin.

"I think it's a rare thing…my work." Her expression went flat. "I'm so busy. And…I was hurt."

"Hey," Chase said softly. He cupped her cheek. "I'm sorry."

"No. It's okay. It's just…you have to know when I say I'm not usually like this, I really mean it. I'm kind of closed. I work a lot. But when I'm down here?" She paused, a sad smile crossing her face, "I can forget it all. Asshole exes. Bullshit bosses. Working a million hours to try to advance my career."

"We all have baggage. Stuff that holds us down."

"Yeah, but the way you live life on a daily basis, it doesn't seem different than vacation. Doing what you want. Even the sex. And this between us…I'm terrified, because it's not something I do. Letting go. What I just did." She felt her cheeks heat and she put her hand to her forehead, coming to terms with the fact that she'd just given him a blow job without even thinking twice. "And it feels good. I just…"

"Penny, it's going to be all right. All of this. I swear it."

Her chest constricted as he lightly kissed her lips. Never making an attempt to deepen it, he hugged her to his chest.

"I don't know where things are going between us but you don't need to be afraid." He pulled away, his eyes locking onto hers. "Let's have fun tonight. This is our second date, after all."

"I guess." She gave a soft laugh.

"How about we continue our sleepover? Get to know each other? Nothing you say or do is wrong. You don't need to be ashamed. I will never judge you." He kissed her forehead and met her eyes. "How are you feeling? Like you're a little out of control?"

Penny nodded.

"Maybe it's life letting you know that whatever you were doing in New York was maybe not as great as you thought it was. Sometimes we have to push way outside our comfort zone before we realize what's really important. Listen, I don't know what we'll discover this week, but I promise you we're going to have a helluva vacation. I have plans for you, mermaid." He smiled.

"You do?"

"Yes, I do. I think the food is here, so let's get on with our slumber party. Okay?"

"Okay," she agreed.

Penny barely registered the water dribbling to an end. He wrapped a warm towel around her, gently dabbing the water from her face and hair. She turned as he held out a robe, and she pressed her arms into the sleeves. Dressing her, he tied it closed.

Falling, falling, falling, Penny thought as she fell into Chase's arms. Like a ball of tightly wound string, she was coming apart. With each small experience, she began to wonder what she was doing with her life. How could she be so incredibly happy in a matter of a day, all from meeting a stranger? But the bigger question, she knew, was how could she return to her bland life, going back to the grind, never feeling this way again?

Chapter Eight

"Truth or dare," Chase suggested.

"You're crazy, you know that." Penny rested back into the bed and crossed her legs. Chase sat on a chair, next to the rolling dining table. An enormous silver tray of crudité and caviar sat chilling on its surface.

"We could move directly to spin the bottle?" He raised a devious eyebrow at her, and picked up the champagne bottle.

"Truth or dare it is," she laughed. "You do have a persuasive way about you. Maybe you should have been a lawyer."

"Perhaps. Maybe a second career? Open," he instructed, holding food to her lips.

She did as he said, smiling as she accepted the cream cheese and caviar. She accepted a flute and took a sip of the bubbly treat.

"Rules are…no talking about work. Anything else is fair game. Also, let's change this game up, I don't remember exactly how this is played, but let's ask the questions first this time. Then you can decide whether or not to answer….go for the dare."

"Fair enough," she agreed. "As much as I like games, I want to get to know you."

"Exactly." He winked. "You go first. Go ahead. Ask me anything."

"You sure?"

"Yep."

"Do you have a girlfriend? And have you ever been in love?" Penny shouldn't have asked, she knew. But something drove her to find out more about the man who was causing her to rethink her entire life.

Chase coughed on his champagne, nearly spitting it out, and held up his hand.

"Dr. Abbott doesn't like being questioned? Remember you said I could ask anything, and I am a professional." She smiled.

"Well, first of all, that's two questions but yeah, I should have known better than to play this game with someone who questions people for a living."

"I'm not sure we're even playing right. We can quit," she suggested.

"Oh no, darlin'. You're not getting out of this so easily."

"Me? I asked the question."

"But my turn is next. So before you give me an out, I'll answer you." Chase picked up a carrot and held it in the air. "Have I been in love? Yes. With Megan Price in seventh grade. I had a huge crush. She broke my heart. It was devastating."

"Be serious."

"I assure you I am. She had the most gorgeous thick red hair. But for some reason she liked my friend, Matt, more than me."

"Do I need to redirect?"

"Okay, okay," he chuckled. "Have I been in love with an adult? I suppose. I do have an ex. We lived together. Never been married, though."

"Are you still in love?"

"Would I be here with you? Of course not."

"But you were in love?"

"Honestly, looking back on things? I'm not sure it was love. Did I tell her I loved her? Yeah, but it didn't seem that way. I'm not sure if I believe in soulmates, but if that's real, I know I haven't ever had that. You know…someone who you wake up thinking, 'I can't live without this person in my life.' When Raine and I broke up, I just think I should have felt more than I did."

"How did you feel?"

"Part of the reason we broke up is because I travel a lot and she likes staying in one place. It was more than just traveling, though. It was a philosophical difference. I enjoy traveling, immersing myself in different cultures, learning new things. Don't get me wrong, it's not that I don't plant roots. I've lived in California most of my adult life. I've got a condo on the beach, and when I'm there, I wake up and look at that beautiful ocean, and it's amazing. But I don't necessarily feel the need to be there all the time in order to maintain my friendships. When I have kids…"

"Kids?" Penny hadn't meant to sound so surprised. She hadn't asked his age, but guessed he was in his mid-thirties. At twenty-eight, it wasn't as if she hadn't heard her own biological clock tick every now and then. But whenever the sucker sounded, without a husband, she'd smacked it down and thrown it across the room.

"Sure. Not now, but someday I want kids. We'll travel places on vacation together. I want to teach them to appreciate other parts of the world, not just our tiny slice." Chase averted his gaze and rimmed his glass as if he'd said too much. "How about you? Have you been in love?"

"Someone cheated on me." She sighed, debating how much to tell him. "I guess I was like you in that I don't think I loved him, but when it happened, I was shocked, angry. He basically called me out on how I'm not available. So I guess even though I wasn't that sorry to see him go, I was still hurt. And it just made me realize that maybe I have to choose."

"Choose?"

"Yeah, I chose work over him. My ex is a jerk, but he was right that I just wasn't around. I've always felt like what happened was my fault."

"No way, Penny. There's no excuse for cheating. He sounds like an asshole to me."

"Can't argue with that." She gave a small laugh.

"I'm very sorry you were hurt, but his loss is my gain." Chase took a sip of his drink and eyed Penny thoughtfully. "My turn. You ready?"

"I'm ready."

"Tonight on the beach...you seemed intent on letting me know that you don't do this. Almost as if you were embarrassed." He held up a piece of cantaloupe to his mouth and sucked off the dripping juice. She smiled and opened her mouth, accepting it. "Tell, me, Penny...do you enjoy indulging outside of vanilla? Because even though I could see you might not have ever been to a nude beach or made love in public, you seemed to enjoy it every bit as much as I did. So that leads me to think you might want to take things a little further."

"Truth?"

"Unless you want a dare?" He smiled.

"No, okay. Truth? I don't know. Tonight, I felt like a teenager or something."

"Except we aren't."

"It was exciting." Penny looked at her fingers, uncomfortable with her thoughts. "I've never been super-adventurous in bed with anyone. I'm the kind of person who's always in control. In my defense, I have to be. It's not like I have room to screw up with what I do. Being down here...with you...it's like a switch has gone off. Somehow it was okay to just let go...but only with..."

"What?" He grinned.

"It's stupid. We've only known each other for a day."

"Tell me."

"I've never met anyone like you. It seems like even though you have this important job, which reminds me, you still haven't told me where you work..."

"I haven't, but that's only because I'm doing work that requires clearances."

"Okay, well, it's the reason you're here though. The fact that you risk your life, diving down to the depths you do…it's not like everyone does that. You're not just adventurous, you seen like an adventurer. My idea of adventure is riding the subway at night."

"Perhaps I need to be a little more specific with my question."

"How's that?"

"Sex, Penny. You seemed to get turned on, knowing someone could watch us."

"Maybe."

"Would you like to watch another couple? Or do you just like being watched?"

"Why do you ask such hard questions?"

"Just want to get to know what you like, is all." Chase held a strawberry to her lips.

"Not sure if I want to watch, but the idea of being watched was exciting." She accepted the fruit into her mouth, licking his fingertip. "But it may have just been the idea of it. If it actually happened, I'm not sure. I can't believe I'm telling you this."

"Do you like to play with toys?"

"Do I own a vibrator? Why yes I do, Dr. Abbott. It's not like I haven't been to an adult store with my girlfriends. But never with a boyfriend. And it's not like I've tried anything crazy." Penny's cheeks heated as she confessed.

"Would you like me to use a toy on you?" He winked.

"Chase...oh my God." She sighed and laughed. "Well, let me say that I'd be open to it. Not sure what you have in mind. But you make me want to try new things...I want to do them with you."

Chase gave a broad smile as if he'd been given a gift, and she wondered if she'd opened Pandora's Box. But it hadn't been a lie.

"I'm looking forward to exploring with you. Let's see what you enjoy." Chase trailed his fingers over her calf.

"My turn." She quickly changed the subject. His hands on her skin was all it took to arouse her, and she was afraid she wouldn't make it through another round.

"Besides sex, what do you do for fun?"

"I love being at the beach, but I think we established that." He laughed. "When I'm not there? I'm in a club of sorts, Altura. There's a group of us. We do all kinds of things. Skydiving, climbing. Love skiing too. I like being outdoors."

"And doing dangerous things, apparently."

"It's not like I'm intentionally trying to put myself in danger. But there's a rush you get. Like going on a roller coaster."

"An amusement park is slightly different than skydiving or scuba diving. I could never do it," she replied.

"Have you ever tried it? Skydiving? Scuba diving?" he challenged.

"Well, no, but I don't think..."

"Did you think you'd be having sex on a beach? A

nude beach?"

"Well, no, but it hardly compares."

"It's the same kind of thing. Maybe not exactly but when I dive...yeah, there's a risk, but take scuba diving, for example. I'm seeing part of this world that not many people get to see. It's not taboo, like what we did, but that adrenaline you felt on the beach? That's what I feel when I dive or skydive. It's pretty awesome. Never say never." He winked

"Have you ever been to New York?" Penny changed the subject but as the question slipped from her lips, she wished she could retract it. Penny wanted more of Chase, and not just for a few days.

"I have," he answered with an amused lilt in his voice.

"And?"

He laughed. "I've been mostly on business. But if you're asking me what I think of the city? I love visiting."

Penny grabbed a cracker and shoved it in her mouth before she asked him anything else. Of course he'd never move there. Embarrassed, she waited on him to go next.

"Would you ever considering living somewhere else besides New York?" he asked.

Penny grabbed a napkin and wiped her mouth. Her eyes met his and she considered what she should tell him. Was he asking her if she'd move to California? *There is no way he's asking me to move there.* Penny tried to rein in her infatuation. She knew she'd say yes, probably scaring the man to the hills. *Don't answer. Don't answer. Don't answer.*

"Dare," she responded, her lips tight.

"Dare, huh? All right." He laughed and stood from his chair.

Penny's heart raced as he moved to the end of the bed and wrapped his hands around her ankles. A small smile formed as he spread her legs, climbing onto the mattress. His hands fell to the ties of her robe.

"Tomorrow."

"Don't I have to do the dare now?"

"I'm changing the rules. I have immediate plans for you that can no longer wait." He gave her a devious grin.

"Hmm…you're making me a little nervous."

"Don't worry, I'll always take good care of you."

"You seem to be doing well so far." She took a deep breath as he untied the wrap. Never taking his eyes off of her, he exposed her bare form.

"Scuba diving. You. Me. First, I'll teach you in the pool, and then the next day, we'll go for a short dive."

"No," Penny replied without thinking. She went to shove up onto her arms but he gently placed his hand on her stomach, holding her in place.

"Yes."

"Are you crazy?" she asked, wavering between terror and arousal. The ache between her legs decided the latter. "Did you forget I almost drowned?"

"No, I did not. I told you snorkeling could be dangerous for beginners."

"And scuba diving isn't?"

"Not when you're with your own personal divemaster. I promise to keep you safe." Chase reached for a piece of mango and held it up in the air.

"A master?"

"The very best. I have a feeling you'll be a very good student." Chase gave a wicked smile, dragging the small piece of fruit down over her belly.

"I….ah," Penny gasped as he brought the slippery fruit through her mound. She watched with fascination as his head dipped between her legs. "Yes."

"See, I knew you'd say yes."

As his tongue hit her clit, Penny gripped the sheets. The warmth of his mouth paired with the cool fruit on her hot flesh sent her wild with desire.

"Fuck, yes," she responded. She could drown tomorrow and she decided she'd have already gone to heaven.

"That's the spirit, darlin'."

"Chase…"

Penny sucked a breath as two thick fingers filled her channel, curling up into her sensitive ridge. As he lapped at her hooded pearl, her body trembled. She wrapped her legs around his shoulders, tilting her hips to his mouth. His lips sucked at her clit, hurling her over the edge. She cried out, her climax rushing over her. She'd never come so hard and fast in her life.

Within seconds Chase had sheathed himself in a condom. As he swiped his cock through her slick pussy, the remaining spasms of her orgasm rippled through her. The intensity in his eyes told her he, indeed, was a master and she'd willingly submit to his lessons.

Slowly he rocked in and out of her, his thick shaft expanding her core. She lost herself in the moment, her eyes focused on his. *This man will wreck me*, she thought. As his thumb brushed over her clitoris, she moaned and clutched the sheets. With each stroke to her delicate bud, her climax crested. Drenched in arousal, her pussy clenched around his cock, quivering in release. She reveled in the pleasure, but as he pulled out, she protested, unsure of his intent.

"Hands and knees, darlin'," he ordered.

Her eyes widened. At his commanding tone, a fresh jolt of excitement tingled down her spine. She complied as his strong hands turned her onto her belly. Before she had a chance to push up, he'd pulled her hips to him.

"Chase," she breathed. Penny clutched at the pillow, bracing herself.

"Ah...wow, look at this." He caressed the globes of her ass. "Tell me, darlin'. Would you like to be spanked?"

Penny bit her lip, unwilling to admit her desire. As his fingers penetrated her core, she mewled.

"I think that might be a yes. We've got plenty of time for that this week, but right now..." Chase removed his hand, guiding his cock to her entrance. "I need to be in you."

"Yes," Penny moaned as he thrust inside of her. "That's it."

"This," he grunted, continuing to pump in and out of her. His wet fingers circled her puckered flesh.

"I haven't..." she began, startled by his touch. As he

circled her tight hole, she grew hot, wishing he'd penetrate her.

"It feels good?"

"Oh God." She dropped her forehead into the covers, embarrassed. As he continued to touch her, she relented. "Yes…oh God, oh God….I, uh…"

"Relax, darlin'." Chase slowly worked his thumb into her anus, rocking gently back and forth into her. "So beautiful."

"It feels…I know it's wrong but oh, yes. Chase…deeper. Please don't stop."

"That's it…just let go. Enjoy the feel of me in you…in all of you." He wrapped his other hand into her hair, fisting it, lifting her head back to him.

Penny submitted to his dark intrusion, the fullness overwhelming her senses. She arched her back, moving to accept him.

"Harder," she cried. "Fuck me harder. Now!"

Chase did as she said, slamming into her. She accepted him into her, the force jarring her forward. Flesh meeting flesh resounded in her ears. She gave a ragged gasp with each thrust, her channel fisting his rigid shaft.

"Shit, I can't hold much longer."

He released her hair and reached around her torso.

"Oh my God, yes, yes, yes…" she repeated, unable to keep her climax at bay.

"That's it, baby, fucking come with me now. Oh yeah."

He pounded into her, and she splintered out of

control. Screaming his name over and over, she shook, ecstasy claiming her. Penny clawed at the pillow and fell forward into the sheets. She heard him grunt as he came. Like a comforting blanket, his powerful frame covered hers.

Floating in the afterglow, she was barely aware of him removing himself. She rolled onto her side, bunching the covers up to her chin. He returned, spooning her, his warmth enveloping her. As he pressed his lips to her temple, her heart pounded, her thoughts swirling with emotion. Wishing for something she couldn't have, she shoved the errant thoughts into the depths of her mind. As she drifted into sleep, she dreamed of her lover, one who belonged to her, not only for a vacation, but a lifetime.

Chapter Nine

Chase studied Penny's expression as the boat sped over the azure water. Ever since breakfast, she'd been withdrawn, and he wondered what was going on in her beautiful mind. He questioned if he was being selfish for asking her to indulge in his passion after she'd nearly drowned. He knew she was nervous, but she'd bravely learned the scuba basics. The previous day, she'd been the quintessential student at the pool, following his every instruction.

Chase had ordered her custom scuba equipment, so she'd be as comfortable as possible when she went for her first dive. One phone call to the concierge, and she had brand new gear, a warm water wetsuit specified to her size. He hadn't told her that it was a gift, but she'd learn soon enough.

He recalled how they'd made love the first night. Their game of Truth or Dare had given him an insight into the alluring woman who had drawn his fascination. When he asked her if she'd consider moving, he'd been surprised that she'd chosen a dare over revealing her answer. He wondered about her reasons for refusing to tell him, but he hadn't given up on discovering the truth.

Guilt seized his conscience for even allowing the idea to seed. He'd known her all of three days, and he'd become slowly obsessed with figuring out a solution to the quandary of their location issue. The days would pass quickly and he'd have to say goodbye. But unlike when he broke up with his ex, someone who he'd lived with for over a year, he missed Penny already. The stab of regret had already begun to tear into him, and he considered once again that he should stop seeing her.

But as she glanced back at him, her long hair adrift in the breeze, his heart caught, and he was reminded that there was so much more to discover about his mermaid. Not only did he want to know her, the need for her to know him had rooted. He looked to Evan, who shook his head in disapproval. It wasn't as if his friend didn't like Penny. But after Chase opted to teach a novice the ropes instead of going on research dives, Evan expressed concern that he was becoming too involved with her. Chase shrugged off his objections, reminding him that they had already collected samples.

The engine cut to silence and the boat bobbed in the gentle swell. Chase's eyes fell on Penny, who smiled at him. She leaned back into the sun, her palms flat on the deck, bracing herself. He admired how her royal-blue bikini accentuated her every delicious curve.

"We're good," Evan called, drawing his attention.

"Penny, you ready?" Chase studied her face, wondering

if she'd changed her mind.

"Not sure if I'm one hundred percent ready, but I trust you." She carefully navigated her way down the steps.

"Listen, I know we did this as a dare the other night," he paused and took a deep breath, "but I'd never make you do something you don't want to do. If you don't want to go, just say the word and we'll relax here on the boat. No worries."

"I'll be fine," she assured him.

"You sure you're okay with this?"

"You don't think I can do it?"

"I know you can do it, darlin'." Chase took her hands in his, bringing them to his chest. "There's nothing I'd rather do than share this world with you. Down there, it's more beautiful than anything you'll ever see. But as much as I'd love it, I want to make sure you're going of your own accord, is all."

Chase glanced to Evan, who rolled his eyes at him. He knew he sounded like a sappy-ass fool, but he wouldn't risk her safety. Her sexy smile told him she wasn't going to chicken out. Although he hadn't seen her practice law, something told him she applied the same tenacity to every aspect of her life. Even if she'd never experimented sexually prior to her vacation, every indication, every caress and touch, led him to believe she'd meet him toe for toe in the bedroom. Like a flower, she bloomed before his eyes, giving him a glimpse into her personality. Both intellectual and playful, her zest for life was apparent in her words and actions. *Two more days. I have to let her go*, he reminded himself.

Switching off his emotions, he attempted to approach their lesson as he'd done with every other person he'd taught over the years.

"You dry?" he asked her.

"Just sunscreen."

"You may want to just towel off, make sure you aren't oily or sandy." He handed her her wetsuit.

"How far down are we going? Do we really need the suits? I see people on TV and they aren't wearing them."

"Yeah, well. Remember fire ball guy the other day? I'm sure he didn't expect that little surprise. At least if you're suited up, there's less of a chance of that sort of thing happening."

"Okay," she responded. Without hesitation, she shoved a foot into the stretchy fabric.

"I know we talked about this at the pool, but I think we should review the rules."

"Yes."

"Number one. Stay with me. Do not wander off to look at something interesting. Obviously, I'll be keeping my eyes on you, but just in case there's a distraction, no swimming away from me, got it?" Penny nodded, and he continued. "You clear on the equipment? If you have a failure, I've got a secondary octo and so do you."

"Yes." Penny flipped off her sunglasses, squinting into the sun.

"Once we get in, we'll double check the equipment. We're going down slow to give you a chance to acclimate.

This is a shallow dive. Fifty feet tops." Chase zipped up and watched as Evan helped her don her gear. "Ascent is the important part. We'll take safety stops on the way up. When I stop, you stop. Okay?"

"Yes, sir," she said, a flirty lilt in her voice.

Holy shit. Chase stopped in his tracks, and raised an eyebrow at her. The idea of her calling him sir as he smacked her ass caused his dick to stir. It took all of ten seconds for the image to form and he was hard. His eyes glanced to Evan, who laughed, well aware of the effect it would have on him.

He scratched the back of his head, and turned to check his equipment. He couldn't recall the last time he'd gone diving with an erection and wondered if his balls would be as blue as the sea when he got out. *Concentrate, asshole*, he told himself.

"Ready?" he bit out.

"Thanks, Evan." Penny gave his friend a smile as he patted her on her shoulder. "Yep, let's do this."

"You can let her go now," Chase growled. He pulled his mask over his eyes, shocked at the jealousy that punched his gut. He must be losing his damn mind, he thought, reminding himself that he'd been dating her for all of three days. "I'll go first. Make sure she gets in okay."

As he spilled into the ocean, he tried to play off his feelings. But he knew he was in the deepest water of his life when it came to his mermaid. With unfamiliar feelings spinning out of control, the best he could do was to let it ride. Of all the risky things he'd done over the years, having a vacation affair with Penny Travis had turned up the dial on what it meant to be an adrenaline junkie. He'd set out treating the situation like an experiment, yet what he'd already learned was that he was in way over his head.

As Penny relaxed into their dive, she grew fascinated with a wondrous universe she had never known existed. When she'd snorkeled, she'd had trouble with the breathing apparatus. Accidentally inhaling water, she'd been deprived of time to view the gorgeous corals. Although she knew scuba diving wasn't without risk, she'd done her best to learn from Chase, and was now enjoying the experience. Within the depths of the Caribbean, she gave over her trust to him.

As he swam by, she mused that he was a master in the sea as well as the bedroom. She was beguiled by his quick-witted conversation; he kept her on her toes with his spontaneous sexual-tinged banter. The more time they spent together, the more she didn't want it to end. In truth, Penny didn't believe in love at first sight. Of a more practical nature, she'd been convinced the concept only existed in fairy tales. Lust seemed a more rational explanation for her feelings, she surmised. But as she contemplated the reasons why she was attracted to her handsome rescuer, she knew it wasn't just the heat of passion that had drawn her to him.

Chemical attractions faded but the true nature of a man didn't. Chase's desire for adventure seemed to be matched with his interest in getting to know her. Their lovemaking sessions were accompanied by long conversations. From favorite movies to family vacation stories, they shared parts of their lives. More than a lover, he'd become a friend, and she couldn't face never seeing him again. Despite her logical nature, she felt herself falling hard for the captivating man who was no longer a stranger.

A dark shadow caught Penny's attention, her daydream coming to a blunt end. A tug on her arm caused her to startle and she caught the look of anger in Chase's eyes through his mask. She immediately knew she'd broken one of his rules, realizing that she'd drifted several feet away from him. Her stomach lurched as he pointed to a large striped shark. The good news was that it appeared uninterested as it swam away. The bad news was that it was a deadly creature and she'd put herself in danger by not paying attention.

Penny was thankful that they were underwater, because if they hadn't been, she was fairly sure he would have reprimanded her. She wasn't convinced he'd forget, however, and expected that when they surfaced, he'd address it. If there was one subject that turned him serious, it was safety. Although he engaged in many dangerous activities, from skydiving to heli-skiing, he'd told her several times that he didn't try to cheat death.

He pointed to a small cave and gave her a thumbs up.

She took sight of the cavern and shook her head, promptly returning his signal with two thumbs down. *No fucking way*, she thought. She had her limits, and he'd just discovered one. Self-preservation had always taken priority over things that appeared fun to other people. Snowmobiling through Yellowstone? *Too cold.* White water rafting with coworkers? *Not happening, I'll drown.* Swimming through a tiny black hole that looked like Barbie couldn't fit through it? *Hell fucking no.*

Penny caught the disapproval in his eyes, and her chest squeezed with guilt. She knew there wasn't much time left, and this might be the only dive she'd ever go on. Chase reached for her hand and brought it to his chest. Her boring routines flashed through her mind, reminding her how he'd breathed vigor into her otherwise mundane lifestyle. His warm eyes brimmed with confidence, and she knew he'd never hurt her. *Trust him.* Taking a chance on love and life, Penny nodded and gave in to her own desire to experience the sea through his eyes.

Acquiescing to adventure, she followed him into the hollow rocks. To her surprise, it was just a short tunnel to the other side. When they emerged, she was stunned at the spectacular sight. Hundreds of colorful fish swam in harmony, brushing around them. What seemed like a blink in time passed before he gestured for them to begin their ascent. After several decompression stops, she broke the surface. Chase already had his mask off and helped her with hers.

"Thank you, thank you so much." Elated, she kissed

him before he had a chance to say a word.

"You liked it?" he asked into her lips, the salty water on their tongues.

"It was unbelievable. I loved it." As she said the words, she wondered what it would be like to say the words to Chase. He smiled at her, and the moment was broken as Evan called to them from above.

"Good dive?"

"It was amazing," she responded, reaching for his hand. As he hauled her up on deck, she panted, trying to catch her breath.

"You okay?"

"I'm good. It was just so…I've never seen anything like it. Chase…he's a great teacher."

"I wish I could say the same for my student," Chase commented.

"I'm sorry. I just…I was distracted."

"What happened?" Evan's tone turned serious.

"Someone drifted away for a few minutes is all." Chase removed his equipment and unzipped his suit but kept his eyes trained on Penny.

"A shark," Penny told Evan.

"A tiger," he added.

"Sounds like maybe you need to do a review with her. Don't want to become fish food," Evan commented. After assisting her with her gear, he turned his attention to the bridge. He fired up the engine, and her eyes met Chase's. "All right then. Time to get back."

"Chase, I didn't mean to…"

"I realize that, but when we go again, I think perhaps we need to find a way to help you remember instructions." His tone was serious, but he gave a devious smile.

"Perhaps." Penny shivered at his stern words, laced with sexual innuendo.

"I'd be happy to help." Evan winked, catching his meaning.

"No. This is my responsibility. The next time she will follow the rules," he promised.

"If there's a next time. Vacation's almost over," Penny baited him, presenting him with an indirect invitation to continue their affair after the vacation ended.

"That it is, but it doesn't mean I'm letting you off the hook," he answered, without giving her any indication that he intended to see her again.

Penny sighed and shoved her sunglasses onto her face, hoping they'd conceal her disappointment. Wishing for something that couldn't happen was ridiculous. She could feel her heart slowly breaking, unsure of how she'd get on a plane in two days. Wrapping her towel around her shoulders, she took a deep breath as the boat sped toward shore. The wind in her hair, she prayed it would blow away the foreboding of sadness in her chest.

Chapter Ten

After returning from the dive, Penny had gone off to have lunch with Tori. Although they hadn't spent much time together, her friend had insisted she'd had a good time. During their conversation, Tori had hinted she wanted to fly out early. One of her ex-boyfriends was in the city on business, and she wanted to see him before he left town. Although Tori had protested, Penny had insisted she'd be all right on her own for the remaining days. With separate hotel rooms, they'd barely seen each other the entire vacation anyway. By the end of the meal, Tori had changed her flight, and had made arrangements to fly home tomorrow.

Home. In two days, she'd return to New York, and everything in her predictable life would fall back into its place. No sand, sun, or cocktails at noon. Her affair with Dr. Abbott would be nothing more than a beautiful memory.

Penny glanced around the small open-aired cabana, and gave the masseuse a smile. The pint-sized woman appeared friendly, but Penny held no doubt that she was a professional, taking notice as her muscular forearms and hands worked the water out of a washcloth.

"You can go ahead and undress," she instructed. "We'll start face down. I'll be right back."

"Thank you." Penny glanced around the room, realizing the small hut provided little privacy. She made quick work of removing her sarong and mounted the table. As she lay on the bed, she took in the spectacular sight of the beach, the sun slowly dropping into the horizon. The sound of breaking waves soothed her mind.

A small towel brushed over her bottom, and she breathed in the sea air. Strong fingers scrubbed her scalp, and within minutes, Penny fell into requiescence. As the masseuse removed her covering, the sensation of the warm sea air teased her bare skin.

Warm oiled hands worked her shoulders and she released an unintentional moan, closing her eyes. Every muscle relaxed as they made their way down her back. Just as she was beginning to drift off into sleep, the massage lingered on her bottom. She startled as fingers delved precariously close to her inner thighs. She turned her head to protest only to find Chase smiling down upon her. His white linen pants were tied precariously low on his hips, and her eyes were drawn to the v cut, his tanned abs, ripped as if they'd been made of chiseled marble.

"What are you doing here?" she asked, her voice sleepy. "Where's the masseuse?"

"She's taking a break."

"Not that I'm complaining, but what did you tell her?" She gave a small laugh.

"I told her we were on our honeymoon and I wanted to surprise you," he responded, with a lilt of amusement.

"What?" Penny clutched the table.

"You know, as in married. You really need to relax." Chase unclenched her fingers from the bed and moved them to her sides.

"And she believed you?"

"As you've pointed out, I can be very convincing," he stated, resuming his work.

"You got me to go scuba diving today, didn't you?"

"That I did. But technically you agreed."

"Oh my God, that feels amazing," Penny moaned, as his thumbs stroked through a knotted muscle. "You could have a second job."

"Miss Travis' personal masseur?"

"You're hired."

"About today, why didn't you listen, mermaid? I know you knew the rules."

"Hmm…sorry. I just was so overwhelmed. Normally I don't lose concentration like that, but it was beautiful. I've never see anything like it."

"It's pretty amazing, huh?"

"I can see why you do it, now. I don't think I could appreciate it before. If you hadn't dared me," she laughed, and continued, "I don't think…no, I know I would have never done it."

"We can do it again sometime," he offered.

"Tomorrow?"

"You can invite Tori if you want."

"Hmm…thanks but she's going home."

"Everything okay?"

"Yeah, she's in an on again off again relationship with this guy. I guess while I've been busy she's been texting him."

"I suppose I've been monopolizing your time."

"Don't worry about her. She's a big girl. Besides, the first night you and I went out, she left the resort to go to some club. I love Tori, but I see her all the time at home. And honestly, this has been the best time of my life," she confessed.

"I can't say I'm sorry to have you all to myself. I just wish…" Chase's words trailed off in reflection.

"What?"

"Nothing…just wish we had more time."

"Me too." Penny's voice grew quiet.

"We should focus on today. Carpe diem, as they say….which reminds me, darlin'."

"What?"

"It's about that spanking we discussed." His hands roamed over her buttery skin, caressing her cheeks.

"Spanking?" Penny's pulse raced, wondering what he had planned. She glanced out the window, where a passerby walked on the beach. "Here?"

"Yes, Penny, right here. As I recall, you seemed to enjoy the idea the other night."

"Did I say that?" She feigned ignorance, her body

craving his touch.

"You were a very naughty diver today." He gave her a wicked smile. "You need to learn that lesson…never go off without me."

"Chase…I'm not sure I'd like…ah," she cried as the first slap landed on her bottom and her core clenched in arousal. Her pussy throbbed and she writhed her hips against the table, seeking relief. "You're evil. Don't tease me."

"Who's teasing? I never start something I don't finish."

"You know someone could see us…ow…ah." Penny quivered as he spanked her again. Just as she was relaxing into the tantalizing pain, his hand slid between her legs, grazing over her entrance. She gasped as he spread her labia, circling his fingers around her clitoris without actually touching it. She both hated and loved how he knew exactly how to turn her on, prolonging her pleasure. "Chase…that…please."

"Begging. That does sound nice, but I think I want to hear you scream my name," he told her, his commanding tone warning her that he was serious.

"I can't…I…" Penny moaned as he penetrated her with two fingers, pumping in and out of her. Her hips tilted into his hand, attempting to bring attention to her aching clit. As he spanked her twice more, her sheath clamped down around him. "Chase! Ah…"

"That's better. And look at how fucking wet you are, darlin'."

Penny pressed her forehead into the table, overwhelmed with her arousal. Being around Chase changed everything she thought she knew about herself. This time, as she took note of a passing couple, she could have cared less. All she needed was him. *Now. Touching her. In her. Forever.*

"Look what you do to me, mermaid. Fuck, I'm hard for you." He cupped his groin, then reached to her. Threading her hair into his fingers, he gently turned her head so she faced him. "Take my cock."

She licked her lips at his order, her eyes meeting his, and tugged his pant strings open. As they fell down, his enormous shaft sprung toward her and she fisted it, running her thumb over its glistening slit.

"Oh yeah, that's it. Suck it, Penny," he ordered as he pressed his thighs against the table.

Penny didn't think twice, submitting to his demand. She guided the plump crown between her lips, licking his seed.

"I've never…ah, Penny. You're fucking amazing."

"This is mine," she told him. The power shifted as she swallowed him all the way down to his root. His fingers went loose, releasing her locks. Penny sucked the length of his shaft and then removed it from her mouth. "Say it."

She flicked her tongue over its head, teasing him. Penny's breath quickened as he plunged into her again. Her core convulsed around his fingers, and she knew she wouldn't last long. But if she never saw this man again, he'd remember that she owned him. He'd never forget her, no matter how far he lived from her.

"Say what?" he grunted.

"Say it, tell me this cock belongs to me," Penny

growled. Somewhat cognizant that she'd gone feral, she pressed his head to her lips, waiting for his response. Something about Chase transformed her into a sultry, wanton woman and the satisfaction of knowing she could make him tremble drove her to give him pleasure.

"Oh God...fuck yeah, this cock is for you, only you, darlin'. Take it...take it all."

"Yes." Penny exhaled, plunging his cock into her mouth.

She rolled to her side, hips rhythmically thrusting as his fingers fucked her pussy and thrummed her hooded bead. A garbled cry escaped her as she seized in pleasure.

"Penny...I'm gonna come," he warned.

Refusing to let him retreat, Penny reached around his hips and dug her fingernails into his ass.

"Oh shit....yes, yes...ah..." Chase bellowed as he erupted.

Sated, she slowly released him from her grip, the tremors of ecstasy subsiding. Penny squealed as Chase slid next to her, bringing her into his embrace. Inhaling his sea-tinged scent, she pressed her lips to his chest.

As she lay in his arms, she knew that while she may have mastered the master, Chase had stolen her heart. The sexual words they'd confessed in passion had meant nothing. Like an illusion come into clarity, she realized she owned nothing. She fought the shroud of melancholy that threatened to destroy their remaining hours together. Closing her eyes, she cuddled against him, yearning for a future with her unattainable lover.

Chapter Eleven

As Chase lifted his glass to his lips, he gazed upon Penny. He'd told her she looked stunning, but words did little to describe her beauty. The elegant blue tie-dyed chiffon swept down her back to her feet, with its mini-dress front revealing her long tanned legs. Over the shoulder draping accentuated her tanned shoulders. As his eyes devoured her, he resisted the urge to touch her sun-kissed skin, leaning back into his chair.

As the band played, her eyes darted to his. Her infectious smile warmed him straight through to his heart, and he began to rethink his experiment. To call it a success or failure couldn't describe what had happened to him. It didn't matter that they'd just met. Penny Travis was not and would never be a forgotten, carefree affair.

While he loved Evan like a brother, they'd fought when they'd returned from diving. Chase had insisted he wouldn't hurt Penny, but Evan argued that she'd already developed feelings for him. He'd played it off, telling him that he and Penny had decided to keep things light. But nothing could be further from the truth. Despite her denials and casual responses, he detected the sadness in her eyes whenever they mentioned leaving paradise.

Chase had been profoundly affected by their dive. Even though she'd lost focus, she'd trusted him completely, allowing him to share with her the exquisite unique environment that few humans were privy to seeing, his world. Unable to let her slip through his fingers, Chase planned to ask her the question again, the very one to which she'd refused to answer; would she consider moving?

It was insane for him to ask, he knew. She'd have no reason to throw away her entire career for a man. But ignoring what he believed was developing into love simply wasn't an option. At one point, he'd agreed with her, telling her he didn't believe in soulmates. But every single time they had a conversation, made love, it felt surreal. Domination turned into submission and back again. Humor melded into heartfelt discussions, where he ended up revealing more about himself to her than he'd ever told anyone. Their last day together was quickly approaching. If he didn't take action, they'd soon be three thousand miles apart with no hope of a future.

The band transitioned into a ballad, and he stood, extending a hand to her. A broad smile crossed her face as she accepted, following him onto the dance floor. He pulled her close, and they swayed gently to the island beat.

"I don't want to go home," he heard her say. Her voice wavered as she spoke.

"I don't want to go home, either, darlin'. But alas, we do have to return to reality."

"This has been the best time of my life," she confessed.

"Penny, this thing between us...I don't want it to end." Chase pressed his lips to the top of her head as they danced. "We're going to have to talk."

"It's complicated."

"That it is."

"We could try to see each other a few times a year. You said you come to New York."

"I do."

"We could Skype. Facetime?"

"True, but long distance relationships are hard on the heart. I can't expect you to date only me when we don't get to see each other."

"Yes," she whispered, disappointment in her tone.

"On the other hand..." Chase stopped dancing and gently tilted her chin up so her gaze met his. He stared into her blue eyes for several seconds as if he were searching her soul. But in truth, he was looking for answers that were already inside him. "I wouldn't...I don't want you seeing anyone else. I want this...us."

"Chase, I don't know how..."

The music grew louder, and people flooded the dance floor. As the din blared around them, Chase only heard the sound of his heart pounding as he bent to kiss her. With passion, he captured her lips, imparting the emotion he'd kept hidden. Penny returned his loving kiss, and he swept his tongue against hers, tasting his sweet lover. In each other's arms, it was as if they were the only two people in the room.

Chase registered the sound of the MC rousing the crowd, his voice booming into the air, and he slowly broke away from Penny. The intensity of the moment didn't falter, however. As Chase's eyes locked onto Penny's, he was certain about his course of action; he'd ask her to move to California. He'd present his best argument to the lawyer who valued logic and set out to win the case and her heart.

Chapter Twelve

As Chase opened the door to his villa, a butler ushered them into the candlelit room. Penny covered her mouth in surprise, taking in the sight of the twinkling lights. Vases filled with tropical flowers adorned every available surface. The scent of Asiatic lilies permeated the air, and she took a deep breath, reveling in the sensation. From red ginger-lilies to orange and blue birds-of-paradises, the plethora of colors created a magnificent floral rainbow.

"You did this?" Shocked, she turned to Chase, who gave her a sexy smile.

"Do you like it?" He beamed.

"Yes, it's unbelievable. Why?" She reached for a bud, sliding its soft petals between her fingers.

"No matter what happens, I want you to know how important this time has been to me. It's not just about the sex either...although that's been pretty spectacular." He laughed, but his smile faded as he took her hand in his. "I've never met anyone like you...ever. Not at home. Not on vacation. I don't know how this will end come

Saturday, but tonight, I want you to know how much you've meant to me."

"Chase…I…" Penny's chest bloomed with emotion, and unexpected tears brimmed in her eyes.

"Hey, darlin'. No tears. This is supposed to make you smile." He brought her palm to his lips.

"Sorry…I just…thank you." She glanced at the flowers, and her eyes met his. "No one has ever done anything like this for me. It's not just the flowers either. It's everything. This week has been the most amazing time of my life. Back on the dance floor. What you said," she paused, and licked her lips, "I wouldn't want to see anyone else. I want you to know that. I know we've only known each other a few days. It's crazy, but I mean it."

"I don't want you to see anyone else, either," he confessed.

"My job…I don't know, when I think about everything we've done this week, how you make me feel, I only know I don't want it to end. I'm not talking about vacation. I mean us."

"I don't want us to end either." Chase wrapped his arms around her, and brushed the tear from her cheek.

Silence hung between them as they gazed into each other's eyes. His soft lips met hers, and Penny's body flared with arousal as he branded her with his scorching kiss. His fingers traveled to her back, unzipping her dress, and it pooled around her feet, leaving her bare. As he swept her into his arms and laid her onto the bed, Penny surrendered to the love she swore she tasted on his lips, yearning to tell him how she felt. The sound of the crinkling protection was all the warning she had before he slowly penetrated her. She moaned into his mouth, delighting in the sensation, and wrapped her legs around his waist, accepting him.

They spoke no words as their bodies communicated the passionate feelings they were both afraid to express, and she lost herself in his love. Penny arched into his thrusts, his pelvis grazing over her clit. As he increased the pace and pressure, her pussy tightened around him, and she shuddered as her climax rolled through her. Simultaneously, Chase came with her, calling her name into the night.

Penny quietly fought the tears she knew would come. She concealed her reaction, focusing on the bright full moon that shone through the windows. Strong arms came around her waist, his lips to her temple, and she brought her hands over his.

"Thank you for tonight…for everything," she whispered.

"I didn't think this could happen on a vacation," he responded as if he hadn't heard what she'd said.

"Neither did I."

"I wasn't looking for someone." Chase took her hand in his, and drew small circles in the palm of her hand with his thumb. "Going back to reality is going to be difficult, for sure."

"Yep. As much as I love what I do, I don't feel like going back to the courtroom." Penny changed the topic, aware that he wasn't talking about work.

"It must be hard working long hours. It's not like I haven't done it, but I'm not always in the office."

"It's not like it hasn't paid off. I'm doing well. At least I thought I was." Penny considered what she was really doing in New York. Was she willing to say good-bye forever, to give up the chance of a lifetime to be with someone she could love, build a future with?

"And now?"

"I don't know. Coming down here, having a chance to step back from it all… I feel like I've been wasting time. The other day, you mentioned kids."

"Yeah?"

"I want kids too, but I had to stop thinking about it. I kept thinking to myself, 'how can you want children when there's no one in your life?' Still, I want a family someday."

"Me too, darlin'."

"But don't you see? That's never going to happen for someone like me if I don't change. Something's gotta give." She sighed, unsure if she should be confessing her innermost secrets to him. "Having some time off…it's given me a new perspective, is all."

"I know how you feel. I think about this vacation and how it's affected me. I've traveled many places, but I've never met someone like you." Chase placed his lips to her hair and spoke softly. "And now that I have, it has me thinking, reconsidering what I'm doing. We may have only known each other a few days, but I'll never forget this. Being here with you…you've changed everything for me."

Penny allowed his words to resonate. They quietly held each other, absorbed in their contemplation. Indulging in her fantasy, Penny closed her eyes and imagined a life with Chase Abbott.

Penny blinked her eyes open, a stream of sunshine warming her face. She reached behind her and fingered the cold sheets. Her disappointment that Chase no longer warmed her body was soon replaced by pleasure as her vision focused on the plethora of flowers. Despite their impending departure from paradise, having to part ways with Chase, she'd never felt so loved by anyone. Instead of trying to rationalize away the million reasons why she shouldn't fall for him, she decided to embrace the situation for what it was.

Sometimes, life couldn't be explained. It was unpredictable, both brutal and generous, and instead of denying the love in her heart, she'd own it. Regardless of her emotions, things would come to a head. Either they'd find a solution, a way to be together, or they wouldn't. If he didn't want to see her after she confessed how she felt about him, it would make no difference to the outcome. With her fragile and vulnerable heart already in his hands, she was helpless to stop the inevitable. After everything

Chase had said and done, optimism ruled her mind.

Penny donned a bathrobe and retrieved a bottle of water from the refrigerator. Chase's whispered voice bled through the screen door, and she wondered if someone was in the villa with them. Something about his hushed tone warned her not to eavesdrop, but curiosity got the best of her as she saw him on the veranda, talking on the phone.

"Raine, I'm not doing this with you now. I told you I was going to be away for a few days. When I get back, we'll work things out," he said. "I'll be home soon.

Raine. His ex-girlfriend, Raine? Penny's stomach lurched, and she hid from his sight, her back against the wall. Her pulse raced as she listened to the conversation.

"No, I'm not lying. I just told you what we did. Evan and I dove the hole. We may go back again today. Yeah, it was cool."

Is he still seeing her? He lied. Oh my God, how could I have been so stupid? Tears pricked her eyes as he continued.

"Yes, I'll see you as soon as I get back. Everything's been arranged." Chase paced. "Sure I miss it, but duty calls." He rested back onto a lounger, pushing his sunglasses over his eyes, and blew out a breath. "Would you stop it, already? I'm not hiding anything. What am I doing down here? What do you think I'm doing? Relaxing is all. Look Raine, I've gotta go. I want to get in another dive before I leave." He took a deep breath and blew it out. "I promise as soon as I get home, I'll take care of it for you. If you don't want to wait for me, call the service.

Yeah, yeah, you know I'm the best."

His laughter resounded through the air as he paused to listen.

"Okay, then you'll wait for me. My flight gets in Saturday night. I'll have time. No, don't worry, we'll do it soon enough. All right now. Take care. Bye."

Penny swallowed the sob that formed in her throat as she tiptoed out of his villa. As soon as she reached her hotel room, Penny called the concierge and arranged for a taxi. By the time she reached the lobby, she had booked a flight home. She slid into the backseat of the cab and shoved her sunglasses onto her face. As the tears rolled down her cheeks, she slowly erected the emotional wall she'd carefully built so long ago. The familiar barrier was like a pair of well-worn sneakers, not terribly attractive but exceedingly practical.

She told herself that broken hearts healed. She'd throw herself into the mountain of work that she knew waited for her. Love was for fools, and she had twice learned the merciless lesson. Chase was wrong. She'd always been an excellent student. It would be a cold day in hell before she ever let herself fall for someone again.

Chapter Thirteen

Chase sat in his office, bouncing the ball against the wall. He'd thought long and hard about why Penny had left him. He'd been an idiot for accepting Raine's phone call. He'd simply been enjoying a fine Caribbean sunrise, watching the waves roll in as the dolphins frolicked in the peaceful morning surf. When his phone buzzed, he'd considered not answering, but with the samples on the way, he'd wanted to make sure they'd arrived. Instead of discussing the specimens, Raine had called to discuss her latest breakup and her need for him to check out a malfunction in her favorite dive equipment.

At the time, Chase hadn't given much thought to the conversation until he'd discovered Penny had gone missing. After several attempts to contact her on her phone, he'd called the concierge to see if she'd arranged for a spa appointment or excursion. When he learned she'd left for the airport, it only took seconds of shock to put the pieces together. He surmised that she'd overheard his phone call, and assumed he was still seeing Raine.

His first instinct had been to hop a plane to New York City, but he soon grew angry that she'd thought so little of him not to even give him a chance to explain. After returning home, he immediately missed her infectious laugh, the warmth of her in his arms. He considered that his experiment had not failed. He'd tested Penny all right. Indeed, she was adventurous like he'd expected. But so much more than that, she'd woven the threads of her being into his heart. On their last night on the island, he'd known on the dance floor he couldn't let her go, and two weeks later, not a damn thing had changed.

Drastic times called for drastic measures. Chase suspected she'd be pissed when she found out what he'd done. He tapped his pen on Evan's desk, silently rehearsing his argument. A knock alerted him to Evan's presence. He stood in the doorway wearing a broad grin on his face.

"It's done. She's here." Evan approached and handed Chase an iPad.

"Excellent." His eyes fell to the screen, his heart pounding as he caught sight of her fidgeting with her phone. "You put her in my office?"

"Yeah, you know Garrett's going to kick both our asses for this. Already have two text messages from him."

Garrett Emerson, CEO of Emerson Industries, was a friend, but he wasn't at all happy that they'd let Penny onto the executive office floor without a valid appointment. The fact that she'd been allowed to stay led him to believe that Garrett wasn't as angry as they'd initially thought. Although Garrett was traveling, he could have put an end to it at any point with one call to security.

"What did you tell him?" Chase chucked.

"What do you think? I told him that you roped me into this half-assed plan to get your girlfriend to move to California."

"Hey, for the record, I did text him and I asked if I could borrow his nameplate from his office"

"And?"

"He had a few choice words for me. But, I guess the good news is that he didn't say no. So we're on."

"Why not just go to New York and get her?" Evan asked.

"Because I want her to see what it's like out here, where I work, my home. If I went all the way to New York, there's a chance she'd have me booted from her office or apartment before I had a chance to talk to her. She's pissed at me." He shrugged. "Honestly, I'm still a little pissed at her, too. The bottom line is that she played it her way on the island and now, I'm playing it mine. No, this is how it's going to have to be."

"What did you tell her?"

"I didn't tell her anything. She's supposed to be meeting with the CEO to discuss her new client," he explained. The head of Emerson's legal department, Ryder Tremblay, had contacted Penny's employer, specifically requesting her assistance on an unnamed project.

"Good luck, man." Evan shrugged and shook his head at his friend.

"Thanks, but I don't intend to fail," Chase responded, shoving out of his chair.

As he strode down the hallway toward his office, he knew he'd be in deep shit with Garrett if this didn't turn out well. But as he glanced to the tablet and caught sight of Penny, he could have cared less about the consequences. What he'd felt for her on vacation had been as real as the floor underneath his feet, and within hours, she'd be his.

Chapter Fourteen

Penny checked her email, irritated her boss had made her fly all the way to the west coast to meet face-to-face with some spoiled CEO. She could have gone the rest of her life and not ever visited California. The second she'd stepped off the plane, a fresh rush of grief had set in, knowing that Chase Abbott lived somewhere in the state. Her epic fail of a vacation had left her heart splayed apart. After she'd heard him talking with Raine, she'd been devastated. Although she'd thrown herself into work, she'd been unable to shake the memory of Chase from her mind.

She glanced around the office, recalling how Chase had carefully avoided telling her where he worked. Given that he'd neglected to mention he was still seeing his ex, she surmised he'd planned on keeping his whole life a secret. After being given the assignment to go to California, she'd googled Chase, but failed to discover anything regarding his employment. Aside from articles regarding high profile technology patents he'd filed, she'd only found him mentioned in the charity columns, referring to him as a wealthy philanthropist.

Penny's eyes fell to the nameplate on the desk, Garrett Emerson, and she wondered what the hell was taking him so long. It was typical of her petulant rich clients, acting as if no one else's time was important but theirs. He probably got off to a late tee time and was wrapping up things at the nineteenth hole.

The sound of the door opening startled her, but she steeled her nerves, refusing to let him see the annoyance on her face. Instead, Penny relaxed into her professional demeanor. By the time the hour was wrapped, she'd have convinced him that the next time they met it would be over Skype.

"Enjoying the view? I'll admit it's not the Caribbean but it's gorgeous nonetheless," Chase commented.

"What are you doing here?" Penny jumped up, dropping her cell onto the floor. Her eyes met Chase's and he gestured to the chair.

"Please sit." It was a command, not a request, his voice low and dominant as if he were angry.

"What kind of a game are you playing? I'm out of here." Tears brimmed in her eyes and she bent to the ground, sweeping her hand underneath the desk. "I can't do this. You…us…why did you…"

A strong hand caught her wrist. She lifted her lids to meet his gaze, and glared at him.

"Your phone." Chase held it up in the air. When she reached for it, he gave her a wry smile. "No, no, no, counselor. I'm keeping this until you hear me out. No more running."

"Jesus, Chase." She yanked her arm out of his grip and sat back into her chair, wrapping her arms around her waist. "What did you do? There's no client, is there?"

"There's a client, darlin' and you're looking at him. I've already paid for your time."

"Are you fucking kidding me?"

"No, this is no joke."

"Are you crazy? You can't do this."

"Do what?" he asked.

"You can't just fly me out here because you want me."

"Yeah, I think I pretty much did."

"Fuck you," she seethed.

"I plan to darlin', but first we have to get a few things straight."

"You want to talk? Are you serious? What is there to talk about? No, don't even answer. I heard you talking to your ex that day, so as far as I'm concerned, there's nothing to say. I don't want to do this." Penny shoved out of her chair but he blocked her with his body. His familiar scent took her by surprise, memories of their time together flooding her mind. She stifled a sob; heartbroken, her words faltered.

"I don't know what you thought you heard that day, but Penny, please." His voice softened and he reached for her, cupping her cheek. She lifted her teary lids to meet his gaze. "You are the only person I've dated for months. And Raine and I? It's been over for years."

"I heard you talking to her," she bit out.

"You heard me talking to her, yes, but she works here."

"Oh God…you work together. Are you kidding me?" She shook her head and exhaled loudly. "I'm so stupid."

"Yes, but I just told you, it's over between us. She's had twenty different boyfriends since we broke up and is probably now on to number twenty-one. That day on the phone…the only reason I even took the call was because we'd just shipped samples. I wanted to make sure everything got home."

"You really expect me to believe that?"

"Yes, I do."

"This is crazy." Penny attempted to curb her anger, but the conversation played in her mind. "You said you were going to be with her…at home. I heard you."

"Yes. My home, as in California. I don't live with her. I haven't lived with her for a long time."

"But you didn't tell her what you were doing. You didn't even mention me. It was obvious she was asking you."

"Jesus, Penny. I was just coming to terms with my feelings about you. Do you really think I was going to tell her how I felt? Did you expect me to tell her that meeting you had been the most earth shattering experience of my life, and I was trying to figure how the hell to ask you to move out here?" Chase took a deep breath and pinned her eyes with his. "I already told you that I don't even think I ever loved her. I meant that. I meant every word I said to you on vacation. You have to believe me. I'm not letting you go again."

Penny struggled to process what he was telling her. She pressed the heel of her hand into her forehead, overwhelmed with the knowledge that she could have been wrong about what she'd heard. Her fragile heart ached for him as she cautiously considered the facts. Why would he bring her all the way to California, to stage this elaborate proposal, if he wasn't telling the truth? It was too much to comprehend how things could have gone so far.

"Why didn't you call me?"

"I just knew that you'd need more than words. And honestly, when I got back, I thought maybe I needed time to figure out what I really wanted. The fact that you'd think I'd do that to you. That I'd sleep with you, lie to you. You didn't even stick around to give me a chance. I was angry."

"I'm sorry… that day…you said you were going to her." Penny tried to back away but he took her hand in his. Her bottom edged against the desk.

"Yes, I did. She needed me to look at her dive equipment. Our group here, we do all kinds of things together. Evan and Garrett, they lead up our sky jumps. I do scuba. And they trust me to look at their gear."

"They can't get someone else?"

"Yes, they can. That's not the point. The point is that if I'm here, I'll do it. But there's nothing between Raine and me anymore…it's over."

Penny gasped as Chase surrounded her, straddling her legs and placing his palms flat onto the desk. His lips brushed her cheek, his warm breath on her ear. Her skin pricked in awareness as the heat of his muscular body emanated onto hers.

"I'm sorry…it's just when I heard you, it sounded like you were still with her. I shouldn't have left, but I just couldn't stay to argue about it. I've been hurt before," she managed. Guilt flooded her chest as she realized she'd misjudged him. "Oh God, I should have known you'd never do that to me."

"You should have but you know what, mermaid?"

"I'm sorry." Penny shivered as his strong hand glided up her back, into her hair. She surrendered, allowing him to tilt her head to meet his gaze. Her neck exposed, she yearned for his lips on her skin.

"I forgive you," he breathed.

"I'm sorry," she repeated.

"These past two weeks have taught me a very hard lesson." He pressed his lips to the delicate skin behind her ear. "I need you here with me…"

"In California?"

"Yes. In California. In my life. In my home."

"Chase…" Trembling, she placed her palm on his chest.

"I've already arranged for you to take on Emerson as a client, so you can continue with your firm. I want you here. Travel with me. Be with me."

"I…" Penny's heart tightened with love for her handsome rescuer as her dream lingered within reach. Everything she had built in New York had been an empty shell of misguided priorities, but he'd made it possible for her to continue working, so they could be together. What he didn't realize was that she would have moved half way around the world to be with him, job or not.

"Say yes," he whispered.

"Yes, Chase, yes, yes." As the confession fell from her lips, Chase kissed her.

Breathless, Penny slid her arms up his back, desperate to touch him. He reached for her knees, spreading her legs apart. As his erection brushed her panties, arousal tore through her. She moaned in protest as his lips tore from hers, trailing down to her collarbone.

"I love you, Penny Travis."

"I love you, too."

"God, I missed you. Never run from me again," he growled.

"Never," she promised.

His fingers slid up her thighs, hooking on her panties. As he tugged them down, she kicked them off, grunting as he speared his fingers into her pussy.

"Missed me?" he asked with a sexy smile.

"Just a little," Penny laughed. She slid her hand down into his pants, and fisted his steel hard cock. "Missed me?"

"Fuck yeah, and I'm about to show you how much."

Penny giggled as he swept his arm across the desk, sending a stapler and pens flying across the room. As he turned her toward the window, she caught sight of the ocean beckoning in the distance. The cool air conditioning skimmed across her wet opening as he hiked up her skirt and bent her over. Her palms flattened against the smooth surface, his knees spreading her wide open. As he donned protection, her heart sped in anticipation. A slap to her bottom caused her to squeal and her breath quickened, his head pressing into her entrance.

"Ah," she cried, as he sheathed himself to the hilt.

"You see that view, darlin'?" He pulled out and slammed back into her.

"Ah, yes." She laughed. "Is this a real estate tour?" Her flippant remark was rewarded with a sharp spank on her other cheek and her pussy contracted around his shaft.

"That is what we are going to wake up seeing for the rest of our lives. You and me."

"Please don't stop," she begged as he increased the pace of his thrusts.

She clawed at the edge of the desk, bracing herself. It had been so long, missing him, loving him. He plunged inside Penny, his swollen flesh stroking her channel. She exhaled as he reached over her, raking his fingers through her hair and bringing his lips to hers. As his other hand found her clit, she moaned in response. His touch set her nerves on fire, her climax building. Penny screamed his name into their kiss, their simultaneous release exploding like fireworks.

"I love you," she heard him tell her over and over.

As the waves of ecstasy subsided, he scooped her into his arms. She kissed his chest as he carried her to a small loveseat that sat across the room. They fell onto it, and Penny smiled, her heart blooming with happiness.

Within his embrace, she quietly celebrated their

reconciliation. A simple vacation affair had transformed into a burning love that wouldn't be denied. She didn't know for certain what their future held, but she knew whatever adventures they forged, they'd explore them together.

Erotic Romance by Kym Grosso

Club Altura Romance

Solstice Burn
(A Club Altura Romance Novella, Prequel)

Carnal Risk
(A Club Altura Romance Novel, Book 1)

Lars' Story
(A Club Altura Romance Novel, Book 2) Coming 2016

The Immortals of New Orleans

Kade's Dark Embrace
(Immortals of New Orleans, Book 1)

Luca's Magic Embrace
(Immortals of New Orleans, Book 2)

Tristan's Lyceum Wolves
(Immortals of New Orleans, Book 3)

Logan's Acadian Wolves
(Immortals of New Orleans, Book 4)

Léopold's Wicked Embrace
(Immortals of New Orleans, Book 5)

Dimitri
(Immortals of New Orleans, Book 6)

Lost Embrace
(Immortals of New Orleans, Book 6.5)

Jax's Story
(Immortals of New Orleans, Book 7)
Coming Fall 2015

About the Author

Kym Grosso is the USA Today bestselling and award-winning author of the erotic romance series, *The Immortals of New Orleans and Club Altura*. In addition to romance, Kym has written and published several articles about autism, and is a contributing essay author in *Chicken Soup for the Soul: Raising Kids on the Spectrum*.

Kym lives with her family in Pennsylvania, and her hobbies include reading, tennis, zumba, and spending time with her husband and children. She loves traveling just about anywhere that has a beach or snow-covered mountains. New Orleans, with its rich culture, history and unique cuisine, is one of her favorite places to visit.

• • • •

Social Media/Links:

Website: http://www.KymGrosso.com
Facebook: http://www.facebook.com/KymGrossoBooks
Twitter: https://twitter.com/KymGrosso
Pinterest: http://www.pinterest.com/kymgrosso/

Sign up for Kym's Newsletter to get Updates and Information about New Releases:
http://www.kymgrosso.com/members-only

Printed in Great Britain
by Amazon